Lying Awake

Lost in Place
The Soloist
The Laughing Sutra
Iron and Silk

Lying Awake

MARK SALZMAN

BLOOMSBURY

First published in Great Britain 2002

This paperback edition published 2003

Copyright © by Mark Salzman 2000

The moral right of the author has been asserted

Bloomsbury Publishing Plc, 38 Soho Square, London W1D 3HB

A CIP catalogue record for this book
is available from the British Library

ISBN   9780747561408

10 9 8 7 6 5 4 3 2 1

Printed and bound in Great Britain by
CPI Antony Rowe, Chippenham and Eastbourne

To Jessica Yu, my north star

1997

God's Mystery

Saint James, Apostle

Sister John of the Cross pushed her blanket aside, dropped to her knees on the floor of her cell, and offered the day to God.

Every moment a beginning, every moment an end.

The silence of the monastery coaxed her out of herself, calling her to search for something unfelt, unknown, and unimagined. Her spirit responded to this call with an algorithm of longing. Every moment of being contained an indivisible—and invisible—denominator.

She lit a vigil candle and faced the plain wooden cross on the wall. It had no corpus because, in spirit, she belonged there, taking Christ's place and helping relieve his burden.

Suffering borne by two is nearly joy.

Fighting the stiffness in her limbs, she lifted her brown scapular, symbol of the yoke of Christ, and began the clothing prayer:

Clothe me, O Lord, with the armor of salvation.

She let the robe's two panels drop from her shoulders to the hemline, back and front, then stepped into the rough sandals that identified her as a member of the Order of Discalced—shoeless—Carmelites, founded by Saint Teresa of Avila in the sixteenth century.

Purify my mind and heart. Empty me of my own will, that I may be filled with Yours.

A linen wimple, with the black veil of Profession sewn to its crown, left only the oval of her face exposed. Mirrors were not permitted in the cloister, but after twenty-eight years of carrying out this ritual every morning, she could see with her fingers as she adjusted the layers of fabric to a pleasing symmetry.

Let these clothes remind me of my consecration to this life of enclosure, silence, and solitude.

She sat at her desk to read through the poems she had written the night before—keeping her up until past midnight—and made a few changes. Then she made her bed and carried her washbasin out to the dormitory bathroom. She walked quietly so as not to wake her Sisters, who would not stir for at least another hour. The night light at the end of the hall was shaded with a transparency of a rose window; its reflection on the polished wood floor fanned out like a peacock's tail.

As Sister John emptied the basin into the sink, taking care to avoid splashing, the motion of the water as it spiraled toward the drain triggered a spell of vertigo. It was a welcome sensation; she experienced it as a rising from within, as if her spirit could no longer be contained by her body.

Wherever You lead me, I will follow.

Instead of going to the choir to wait for the others, she returned to her cell, knelt down on the floor again, and unfocused her eyes.

Blessed is that servant whom the master finds awake when he comes.

Pure awareness stripped her of everything. She became an ember carried upward by the heat of an invisible flame. Higher and higher she rose, away from all she knew. Powerless to save herself, she drifted up toward infinity until the vacuum sucked the feeble light out of her.

A darkness so pure it glistened, then out of that darkness,

nova.

More luminous than any sun, transcending visibility, the flare consumed everything, it lit up all of existence. In this radiance she could see forever, and everywhere she looked, she saw God's love. As soon as she could move again, she opened her notebook and began writing.

Martha

Mother Mary Joseph, the former prioress, kept her hands folded under her scapular and her gaze lowered. She walked close to the wall so as not to draw attention to herself even though no other Sister was present. In spite of being nearly doubled over from osteoporosis and weakened from a recent bout of pneumonia, she still joined the choir for all of the canonical Hours. In religion for sixty-one years, Mother Mary Joseph was a Living Rule, a nun who epitomized the highest ideals of contemplative life. Tradition held that if the laws and constitutions of the Order were ever lost, they could be recovered simply by watching a Living Rule pray.

She lowered the wooden clapper from its place on the wall but felt, as always, reluctant to cleave the Great Silence. God's mystery roared in her ears. The cool, still air felt good against her cheeks, and she gave thanks for that. In a few hours the sun's heat would test her fortitude, but Mother Mary Joseph thanked God for trials, too. Gratitude must know no limits.

She struck the clapper hard.

More than just a summons to devotions, it was the voice of Christ calling to His servants. Any Sisters who were not already up answered with their knees as they dropped to the floor in their cells.

"Praised be Jesus Christ and the Virgin Mary, his mother. Come to prayer, Sisters, come to praise the Lord."

Mother Mary Joseph struck the clapper a second time, then returned it to its place on the wall. She descended a shallow staircase, lifting her habit from the rear to prevent it from brushing against the steps. Causing the fabric to be worn unnecessarily would be a fault against the vow of poverty. Her sandals whispered across the parquet floor, then she stepped into the courtyard.

It was still dark outside. The hush of predawn traffic drifted up the canyon and over the cloister wall. The world had closed in on the monastery since its construction in 1927. With the Golden State Freeway to the east, Chinatown to the south, the Police Academy to the north, and Dodger Stadium a mile to the west, the Sisters of the Carmel of St. Joseph now prayed from the very heart of Los Angeles. Still, tucked in a fold of hills at the end of an unmarked driveway, the monastery was as invisible as a sunken ship.

The one-story buildings of the cloister spread out to form a U, with the open end facing west, up into the canyon. The main building housed the chapel and choir, the bell tower, the refectory, and the kitchen. The northern arm held the common room, the visitor's parlor, and the scriptorium. The other had been divided into private cells for the nuns. Eaves of thatched mesquite provided shelter from the sun as the Sisters moved from one part of the cloister to another. Every fall, the youngest Sisters climbed up on ladders and laid plastic sheets over the eaves for protection during the rainy season.

A masonry wall extended up into the canyon, sealing off the enclosure and giving them half an acre of property for walking, gardening, and contemplation. At the far end of this property, hidden by mulberry trees and a thicket of bamboo, two hermitages offered privacy for Sisters who felt the need for even deeper solitude than the regular schedule provided.

Skirting under the eaves, Mother Mary Joseph entered the choir and turned on the lights, dimming them to the intensity of candlelight. The empty wooden stalls, where the nuns sat and stood to pray, faced each other in two rows from opposite sides of the room. Mother Mary Joseph genuflected before the altar, then crossed the room to her own stall, from which she had prayed for more than half a century. She removed her Liturgy of the Hours from under the seat and used colored ribbons to mark the pages for the chanting of Lauds; her devotions had worn the gold leaf on the edges of the pages to a dull brown.

The nuns met in choir seven times a day to pray the Divine

Office, the liturgy of the Church. Unlike private prayer or sacred reading, the Office was meant to be recited in public and out loud, so that the written word of God could be turned into a living encounter with the Word that is God. As Mother Mary Joseph prepared her breviary, the others floated into the room like apparitions until all were in their stalls except for Sister John of the Cross. No one broke discipline to stare at the gap in the row of seated figures, but every nun felt the absence. Nothing was more precious to the community, or to the Church, than a Sister's voice and heart in choir.

Mother Emmanuel, the Superior of the monastery, gave the benediction. She called upon all created things to praise their Maker, glancing one more time at the empty stall, then toward the door. Her lips moved silently, then she raised her chin and signaled for the recitation of the Divine Office to begin.

Lord, open my lips.

Then the antiphon:

I have openly sought wisdom in my prayers,
and it has blossomed like early grapes.

The two sides of the choir called out to each other like bridegroom and bride, separated by fate and longing for each other. Gregorian chant, sung in unison without harmony, drifted over the screen hiding the nuns from chapel, then rose toward the heavens, joining the prayers of contemplatives everywhere whose vocation was to pray on behalf of those either unwilling or unable to pray for themselves. During the Office of Lauds, those souls caught in the struggle against temptation were particularly vulnerable, since the rest of the world was still asleep and not praying for their salvation.

The Sisters bowed at the *Gloria Patri*. As they rose, Sister John of the Cross appeared in the doorway looking weary but exhilarated. Several of the nuns glanced at her, unable to mortify their curiosity. Sister Anne, who considered observance of the Rule to be of more value than all extraordinary states, kept her eyes on her breviary and resumed the chanting of the liturgy on her own, forcing the others to catch up.

> *God, come to my assistance.*
> *Lord, make haste to help me.*

Without needing to be told what was required of her, Sister John prostrated herself facedown on the floor of the choir, her arms outstretched in the manner of the crucifixion. Even penance was love.

Ignatius of Loyola

Sister John and Mother Mary Joseph sat opposite each other at a cherrywood table covered with boxes of handmade paper, bottles of colored ink, tubes of paint, jars filled with sable brushes, and a stand for her pens and pencils. A parishioner had donated the table after it had been water-damaged. The Sisters had stripped and refinished it, then given it pride of place in the scriptorium. They dubbed it the Ark because so many precious objects were crowded onto its surface.

Mother Mary Joseph had been working for several days on an illuminated page for Father Aaron's reading at Mass on the Feast Day of Saint Christopher. Her illustration showed the saint carrying a child on his back across a storm-swollen river. She brushed the final touches of gold on the child's hair, blew a few times on the page to stiffen the paint, then handed it to Sister John of the Cross for the copying out of the text.

Start here, end there, Mother Mary Joseph indicated through hand signals. Speech was permitted in the cloister only during the recreation periods following dinner and evening collation.

The sermon, written by Father Aaron for the occasion, described the saint's efforts to keep the child from being swallowed up by the river:

The rain stung his eyes and forced them closed, the waves splashed up over his head, making him choke and gasp, and his legs, which had been carrying people to safety all day, seemed about to give out. And still, the waters rose higher! At the point of despair, he thought of the child on his shoulders and knew he had to fight on, he had to reach the other shore, no matter what.

Sister John could see the river in her mind as she copied out the text, and she understood the saint's anguish. She knew what it was like to feel abandoned by God. She had languished in the cloister for years, her prayers empty and her soul dry, until grace came and brought the drought to an end. When the story finally brought Saint Christopher across the river, and he fell exhausted into the mud, Sister John had to put down the pen to read through to the end:

At last the child revealed himself to the poor giant as Christ, and he said, "You carried the weight of the whole world on your back when you carried me." Sometimes we all feel that way when we share Christ's burden, we feel we are drowning in the sorrows of the world, but if we ask God for the strength to endure for the sake of others rather than just ourselves, we discover how powerful love really is.

Her eyes welled up. This was not just a story to Sister John, it was sacred reading. God spoke to her through these words and evoked, from the center of her being, a response of surrender and gratitude. Mother Mary Joseph watched her and thought: God showers this one with graces.

The monastery bell tolled, summoning the community to midday prayer. Sister John rose to her feet; the copying would have to be completed later. The two nuns filed out of the scriptorium and followed the bare corridor toward the choir. At a turn in the hallway, Mother Mary Joseph stopped, noticed something, then flashed a smile. Lost in the emotion created by the parable, Sister John had forgotten to remove the paper napkin she had tucked under her chin to protect her habit. The two nuns exchanged a glance, then shook with noiseless laughter.

AUGUST 6

Transfiguration

I cried out, and the Lord heard me.

Sister John held her breviary out in front of her, not allowing her elbows to sag or rest against her sides. She welcomed the pain of her headache, knowing that those who love more want to suffer more, in imitation of Christ's difficult life. The stained-glass window on the south side of the choir, an abstract pattern of yellows and oranges and Indian reds, burned a knife-edge of color into the floor near the wall. She listened as Sister Miriam, a novice preparing to make First Vows, read aloud:

My soul is waiting for the Lord,
I count on His word.

My soul is longing for the Lord
more than watchman for daybreak.

Sister Miriam did everything deliberately, as if under constant examination. After three years in the cloister, she still seemed unsure of herself. Her tentative manner and novice's white veil reminded the others of a bird in adolescent plumage.

Expectant silence.

Sister John emptied herself for the voice of the Holy Spirit, letting it resonate within her, turning her heart into a cathedral. The text of the psalms led her, day after day, year after year, through the cycle of life. It looped endlessly, but also spiraled inward, bringing her closer to the mystery of God and the meaning of their lives in God.

The full choir chanted the prayer:

All-powerful and ever-living God,
with You there is no darkness,
from You nothing is hidden.
Fill us with the radiance of Your light.

After the last note had died away, the Sisters filed out of the choir for Sext, the examination of conscience. Sister John made the short journey to her cell, walking slowly because of the headache, then closed the door behind her and faced the simplicity of the room: light, air, and cross. She sat down in her chair, closed her eyes, and reviewed the day and the motivations for her actions.

Have I acted and spoken with God's presence in mind? Have I been grateful for my trials as well as my consolations? Have I lived up to my commitment to trust in God's love completely?

A mockingbird sang in the heat. Sister John heard the sky in its voice.

Cicadas, the rustle of eucalyptus leaves; the music of sun and shade.

Sister John opened a fresh notebook and began to write. Adoration welled up through the pain, closing the gap between lover and Beloved. The force of his presence curved eternity in on itself; it was not her love rising after all, but his love pulling her toward him. She fell upward into brilliance, where all suffering was released.

In the fire of his embrace, all that was her ceased to exist. Only what was God remained.

I am

The cloister bell, the voice of Christ.
He spoke again:

I am

She tried to obey but was frozen in beauty, like a fly trapped in amber. She could not move.

Nothing exists apart from me.

Self had been an illusion, a dream.
God dreaming.

Assumption

Recreation, the hour of speech and laughter.

The nuns drifted through the garden like sailboats, some in pairs, some by themselves. Sister John paused at the fountain to dip her fingers in the water, then touch them to her lips. Someone had placed a spray of wildflowers at the feet of Saint Joseph, whose statue rose from the center of the fountain to welcome all thirsty visitors. Sister John splashed water over the blossoms so they would last longer. Each drop held an image of the world.

Sister Bernadette approached, dragging a garden hose behind her. She topped the fountain off with water, then she and Sister John stepped back to let the birds drink.

A wren eyed them from its perch in the ginkgo tree. It hopped down, one branch at a time, then made a nervous dash for Saint Joseph's toes. Before it could dip its beak, a shrieking jay dove out of the sun and chased it off.

Sister Bernadette wagged her finger at the statue. "You're not doing your job, pal." Formerly a Dominican, Sister Bernadette had been a schoolteacher for a dozen years, then chaplain at a women's prison for another ten before requesting a transfer to a contemplative order. She turned to Sister John. "Forgive me, but bullies really get under my skin." She aimed the hose at the jay and squeezed the handle.

She grinned at the results, but her smile faded when she saw Sister Angelica burst out of the dormitory and march toward the fountain.

"Did I just see what I thought I saw?" Sister Angelica demanded. "Did you spray a bird with that hose?"

Sister Bernadette looked more annoyed than guilty. "He wasn't letting any of the smaller birds drink. He'll be back soon enough."

Sister Angelica glowered at her. "Birds do what they do because God made them that way, and that's his business. Only people can be cruel." She wheeled around and stalked back indoors.

"She's touchy when it comes to animals," Sister John whispered.

"She's touchy about *everything*," Sister Bernadette corrected.

The real penance in cloistered life, most Sisters agreed, was not isolation; it was the impossibility of getting away from people one would not normally have chosen as friends.

Sister Bernadette sighed, then looked up into the trees to search for the little wren. Sister John saw it first. "He's over there, on the wall."

"I see him. Come on, little guy—no one's going to ambush you now."

The wren flew from the wall to a tree, then to a bush, then to Saint Joseph's head. After a final look in all directions before making himself vulnerable, he dropped to the lip of the fountain and began drinking.

The two nuns stood still until the bird had quenched its thirst, bathed itself, and returned to the ginkgo tree to preen.

Sister Bernadette adjusted the nozzle to a fine mist and began cooling off the rosebushes. A rose petal dropped onto one of the flagstones. It reminded Sister John of sunsets in eastern Ohio, where the sun looked like a disc of copper welded onto a sheet of tin.

"Have you finished your poem for Saint Thérèse yet?" Sister Bernadette asked.

An obscure French nun while she lived, Thérèse of Lisieux succumbed to tuberculosis in 1897 at the age of twenty-five. Before dying, she managed to complete a brief autobiography, *The Story of a Soul*. The message of the book was simple: We needn't fear God, or feel that we must do exceptional things to please him, because he loves the humblest soul as much as he loves the greatest saint.

Not everyone loved the manuscript at first. One prioress read it and huffed that "age and experience would have changed her opinions about spiritual matters." Another declared, "The thought that this manuscript is now free for anyone to read distresses me beyond words." Yet the book went on to earn Thérèse the swiftest canonization in Church history. Now, on the hundredth anniversary of her death, Saint Thérèse was to be made a Doctor of the Church, and the Superior General of the Carmelite Order had invited Sister John to compose a poem for the occasion. He had also requested that she make the journey across the Atlantic to deliver the poem in person, at the Vatican, as part of the celebration. The only other American nun scheduled to address the congregation was an abbess who had survived the Mexican Persecution and gone on to make foundations in Arizona, Nevada, and New Mexico.

"I'm working on it," Sister John said quietly. "What if I get nervous? I've never read in front of a group of people before."

Sister Bernadette laughed and shaded her eyes from the sun. "If you get nervous, they'll be charmed. People like it when artists are shy." She pointed the nozzle up for a moment, creating a miniature rainbow in the sunlight, but the mist drifted back on her glasses. As she took them off to dry the lenses with a handkerchief, she said, "Think of the food you'll get to eat! Even the truck stops in Italy make their pasta fresh. If you don't come back with a menu from every meal, I'll spray you like I did the jay."

Queenship of Mary

The scent of fresh bread greeted the Sisters as they filed into the refectory for noon dinner, the main meal of the day. Each nun stopped in the center of the room to bow toward the cross, then went to her place to stand until after grace had been said. At the signal from the prioress, they sat down and fastened their napkins to their habits.

They sat in pairs at small tables, all facing the center of the room. Mother Emmanuel and Mother Mary Joseph shared a table with a replica of a human skull resting on it, a reminder of everyone's mortality and the insignificance of the austerities they endured now. After the prioress had given the benediction, Sister Angelica took the reader's place at the rostrum and began reciting the day's selection, a passage from Augustine's *Sermons on 1 John*:

The entire life of a good Christian is in fact an exercise of holy desire. You do not yet see what you long for, but the very act of desiring prepares you, so that when He comes you may see and be utterly satisfied.

Sister Miriam began the server's slow march around the table, ladling vegetarian soup into each nun's bowl. The rest of the meal—bread, butter, and a spinach salad—was already on the table. Sister Elizabeth signaled for a spoon for her tablemate by raising her index and middle fingers. A Carmelite never asked for anything for herself in the refectory except bread and water. Sister Miriam signaled back with three taps on the chest—*sorry*—and returned with a wooden spoon.

The nuns made as little noise as possible while they ate, focusing their attention on the reader's voice. The contemplative ideal of keeping one's mind on spiritual matters at all times was never more threatened than while putting food into the body. For that reason, decorum in the refectory was maintained as strictly as it was in the choir; speech was forbidden in that room except during special feasts and nuns' jubilee celebrations.

God means to fill each of you with what is good; so cast out what is bad! If He wishes to fill you with honey and you are full of sour wine, where is the honey to go? The vessel must be emptied of its contents and then be cleansed. Yes, it must be cleansed even if you have to work hard and scour it. It must be made fit for the new thing, whatever it may be.

When the prioress struck the wooden clapper to end the meal, Sister John winced. A headache had begun troubling her that morning during manual labor, and a whole hour remained before private prayer, when she could retire to her cell without drawing attention to herself. She gathered all of the crumbs on her napkin and ate them, a reminder of Jesus' admonition: "Gather up the fragments that remain lest they be lost." To waste anything would be a fault against her vow of poverty.

She followed the others out of the refectory to the Chapter room, where nine chairs formed an open circle for the weekly community meeting. Shelves of books lined the room, their spines arranged by height to form pleasing, symmetrical designs. Under a portrait of the Virgin Mary, true Mother of the community, the Sisters had hung a bulletin board pinned with messages, special intentions, and scriptural quotes for the day.

When they had all taken their seats, Mother Emmanuel held an envelope in front of her and announced that she had wonderful news.

"I received this letter from Claire Bours yesterday. She's asked to join us as a postulant!"

Sister Elizabeth looked like a can of soda that had been

shaken hard, then opened. She popped up from her chair, clapped her hands, and asked, "Didn't I say the letter would come this week? I *knew* it."

"What made you so sure, Sister?"

"Because she's just like I was. Her vocation makes perfect sense to me." A former concert violinist, Sister Elizabeth had given up a career in music to heed the call to Carmel, and felt that this sacrifice only strengthened her commitment to religious life. She walked over to where Sister John sat, and gave her a hug. "You should be feeling so much joy right now!"

Sister John blushed, which made her headache worse. The new candidate had been inspired to look into the Carmelite Order after reading *Sparrow on a Roof,* Sister John's book of essays and poems about contemplative life. Every religious hoped that her life of prayer and penance would benefit others, and to have that hope confirmed was a blessing, but too many blessings received by one person could be a problem. In the spiritual life, individual success often came at the expense of community harmony. "I feel grateful," Sister John said, trying to shift attention away from herself. "We're all so fortunate to have the opportunity to serve."

Sister Anne frowned. "I worry that we're comparing apples and oranges here. Sister Elizabeth was raised Catholic, and sensed a calling for years before she heeded it. Everything is new to this girl—she was only baptized two years ago. And she couldn't be coming from a world more different from ours. She works in *Hollywood*." Sister Anne forced the word out as if it hurt.

A mixture of excitement and apprehension accompanied their discussion of the candidate. It was not just a matter of liking or not liking the woman; did she seem to have a genuine vocation to contemplative life? Did God want her in that particular community? Would she make a positive contribution there, or would she be a burden to the others?

Claire Bours was thirty-three years old, had a master's degree in fine arts, and had worked as a film animator for eight years. In her letters to the prioress, she described a persistent questioning—who am I? why am I here? what is my purpose?—which would not go away in spite of her attempts to resolve it through achievements, travel, and intimacy. She wrote:

Four years ago I didn't even know what a contemplative nun was, and a part of me hopes I am mistaken about this. I have doubts, I admit it. But I feel that I've got to give this voice, whatever it is, a fair chance to be heard.

She had visited the cloister for three days, and had impressed the nuns with her intelligence and warmth. An intriguing candidate, but one who raised inevitable questions. Was her sense of a vocation just a phase? Many successful people go through periods when they wonder, "Is this all there is?" and think about giving it all up for the spiritual life.

Such vocations rarely last, however. Life in the cloister quickly becomes just as prosaic as life in the world—perhaps even more so. Once the person finds herself asking, "Is this all there is?" while peeling potatoes or laundering habits, she usually returns to the world.

"There's no need to rush to a decision," Sister Anne continued. "If her vocation is genuine, a little adversity will only make it stronger."

Mother Emmanuel returned the envelope to the pocket of her tunic. "I agree that things have moved quickly for her, but I like the fact that she admits to having doubts. I tend to be more skeptical of those who say they are absolutely certain. Would anyone else like to share their thoughts?"

"God is calling her," declared Sister Angelica, who was rarely equivocal about anything. "What more do we need to know?"

"You're not concerned that she's leaping from one extreme to another, with no middle ground?" Sister Bernadette asked.

"There is no middle ground when it comes to loving God. It's all or nothing."

Sister Bernadette bristled. "For most people, Sister, it's more complicated than that."

"Maybe it shouldn't be!"

Mother Emmanuel ended the argument by asking for a moment of recollection. These short prayers reminded them of God's presence in every aspect of their lives together, not just their time in choir or their cells. After this interlude, the prioress turned to Sister Miriam and asked quietly, "How do you feel about the new candidate, Sister?"

Sister Miriam looked startled. Novices did not vote on new admissions, so she hadn't expected to be called upon during the meeting.

"A first impression, that's all," the prioress encouraged.

Sister Miriam folded her hands on her lap and said that Claire seemed enthusiastic, intelligent, and charming. The flatness in her voice undermined the compliments.

"Was there anything about her that made you uncomfortable?" the prioress asked. "You seemed to be keeping her at a distance, I thought."

The color drained out of Sister Miriam's face. "She had so little time here, I thought she'd want to spend as much of it as possible with the professed nuns. I didn't want to get in the way, that's all."

Fragile silence. "Mother Mary Joseph?"

The Living Rule smiled. "Good teeth, good manners, sensible shoes. I liked her."

The community cast a secret ballot and voted, six to two, in favor of offering Miss Bours admission.

"No doubt she will need time to put her affairs in order," Mother Emmanuel said. "What a glorious year it will have been, between this and the completion of Sister Miriam's novitiate. We're seeing new growth in God's hidden garden." The others nodded their agreement as the prioress took another envelope out of her pocket. "That wasn't the only good news to come in the mail this week. Sister John is too modest to mention this, but I'm going to embarrass her anyway: her book is going into another printing. We'll definitely be able to replace the roof this year."

The Carmel of St. Joseph traditionally depended on the sale of homemade jellies, greeting cards, and communion wafers to meet expenses, but its economic future had brightened considerably since Sister John discovered her gift for writing.

"None of it is my doing," Sister John protested when the others congratulated her. She felt herself blushing again.

"Don't keep your light under a bushel," Sister Elizabeth advised. "Talent comes from God, but it only bears fruit through hard work."

"One more fruit like that and we'd be able to make a foundation in Tahiti," Sister Christine said. "What are you doing sitting here? You should be in your cell, writing."

Sister John prayed that Mother Emmanuel would conclude the meeting soon. During recreation she could sit in a far corner of the room and pretend to write, without drawing any attention to herself or her malady.

Sister Anne, who changed the subject whenever Sister John's book was mentioned during meetings, raised her hand and asked how everyone liked the high-fiber cereal she had instructed the extern nun to buy for breakfast. Several faces in the room drooped, but the Living Rule coughed politely and said, "It's been a blessing for me, I must say," and at least two other Sisters chuckled in agreement.

"But there is still the matter of the juices," Sister Anne continued. "We have a choice of three juices now, because everyone seems to like a different kind, but the cartons take up too much space in the refrigerator. I'm always having to rearrange things to make space for them. Couldn't we just offer one flavor? *Shouldn't* we, I mean? As a matter of poverty?"

In cloistered communities, where everything must be shared, members sometimes become territorial about objects under their care. It was no secret that Sister Anne, whose fidelity to the Rule was otherwise exemplary, had become fixated on the refrigerator.

"That wouldn't be fair," Sister Elizabeth teased. "Whoever happens to *prefer* that one juice would be denied the opportunity to practice poverty."

Sister Anne—who felt that Sister Elizabeth's sense of humor often crossed the boundary into sarcasm—asked dryly, "What would you suggest, then?"

Sister Elizabeth ignored the edge in Sister Anne's voice. "There's plenty of room in the refrigerator. All you have to do is stack a few things. Has anyone else noticed this, by the way? *Nothing can go on top of anything else in the refrigerator.* It's become part of our Constitution, apparently."

"If things pile up, they go uneaten, and—"

"Sisters," Mother Emmanuel interrupted, "we have only a few minutes left for Faults, so let's vote on the juices and move on."

The community elected to maintain the present number of juices offered at breakfast. Mother Emmanuel struck the clapper to end the meeting and called on the Monitress to take over.

Sister Christine rose and began the ritual of Faults by saying in a voice clear of all emotion, "In charity I accuse Sister Elizabeth of whistling in her cell during spiritual reading, which several of us could hear."

Mother Emmanuel imposed a standard penance of five decades of the Rosary. Sister Elizabeth nodded respectfully toward both the prioress and the Monitress, and the ceremony continued.

Sister Christine proclaimed another Sister for falling asleep during the Night Office and snoring, then accused herself of breaking a dish in the sink in her haste to get outdoors for recreation. Mother Emmanuel accused herself of losing her place during Vespers and fumbling noisily through the pages of her breviary. Their daily life was so carefully orchestrated, and so routine, that the recitation of Faults rarely produced any surprises. When it came Sister John's turn to be proclaimed, however, a ripple of curiosity passed through the room.

"In charity I accuse Sister John of the Cross of being absent in choir for the Office of Lauds on Monday, and for the Office of Vespers on Friday."

Instead of imposing a penance right away, the prioress asked, "Are your headaches occurring more frequently, Sister?"

Sister John hoped no one could tell she was having another. "Yes. I apologize, everyone."

"No one's blaming you, Sister—we're concerned, that's all. Perhaps you should see another doctor."

"Migraines come in cycles, and no one knows why. They're inconvenient, but not dangerous."

The prioress did not look reassured. "You could be doing more to take care of yourself. The other night I woke up at two o'clock and saw light coming from under your cell door. You're pushing yourself too hard."

"I don't feel that I'm pushing myself at all. I'm being pulled." Sister John felt the others' eyes on her. Did they understand? Could they forgive her for enjoying these favors from God?

Mother Emmanuel studied Sister John's face closely, looking for signs of pride or self-consciousness, but saw only determination. Sister John had an extraordinary vocation; there was no question of that. But Mother Emmanuel also knew that spiritual gifts made the soul especially vulnerable to the sin of pride. Was Sister John putting her own interests before those of the community?

"I consider this a matter of obedience," Mother Emmanuel began, taking special care to sound untroubled. The other Sisters, she knew, would be listening for any nuance in her voice that might reveal her personal feelings. Sister John's absences in choir had been on everyone's mind lately. "Obedience includes getting enough rest so that you can participate fully in the life of the community."

Sister John nodded in agreement, making the next part of Mother Emmanuel's task easier.

"Your penance shall be to refrain from using the light in your cell for one month. No more writing at night. I want you to get more sleep."

Sister John's heart sank. Writing had become as important as prayer to her—it *was* prayer—but she also knew that the more perfectly a nun submitted to the will of the Superior, the more perfectly she submitted to the will of God. She directed her thoughts toward her Innocent Spouse, who was executed for crimes he could not commit, and accepted her penance with a nod.

Mother Emmanuel struck the clapper once more and gave the blessing for evening recreation:

O Lord, our God, we are about to spend some time in recreation. May it be for Thy honor and pleasure, and grant that this exercise may enable us to perform the works of Thy service with greater fervor, the same grace we ask of thee, O gracious Queen of Heaven.

Sister John moved her chair near the window, put a notebook on her lap, and closed her eyes. She could not afford to single herself out further by asking to be excused now.

The sounds of conversation filled the room.

Thank you even for this pain, Lord.

"Are you feeling all right?"

She forced her eyes open. Mother Mary Joseph had moved next to her without making any sound. The Living Rule's spine looked to Sister John as if it had been bent from having shouldered Christ's burden for so long; her deformity was a grace, no less than stigmata.

"Everything is as it should be, Mother."

The Living Rule grinned. "You've noticed, too? It's the new cereal."

Dear God, help me bear this—

"Are you sure you're all right, dear? You look very pale."

"Forgive me, Mother . . ."

The notebook fell off her lap.

have mercy

She was sure the blood vessels in her head would give way.

please

Her mind fractured under the pressure. She splintered like broken glass, she became all edges and points and she was sure this had to be death, it had to be the end of everything, then her suffering blinked off.

an invisible sun
a shock wave of pure Being
swept my pain away, swept everything away
until all that was left was God.

Nothing outside of God, nowhere exists outside of God.
His presence is the only reality; the nightmare of suffering dissolves in the light of truth.

God awakening.

Beheading of John the Baptist, Martyr

A knock from outside the enclosure, the signal that the car was ready. Sister John knelt before Mother Emmanuel, who delivered the prayer for a nun leaving the cloister:

May the Virgin Mary and her loving Child bless and keep you and bring you safely home.

When the prioress opened the heavy oak door, the hinges cried in protest. "You'll be in all of our prayers today, Sister."

Sister John kept her eyes lowered. "Peace of Christ, Mother."

The door cried again as it shut behind her.

Sister John felt each stone through her sandals as she stepped out onto the gravel driveway. Leaving the enclosure made her feel uneasy, like being caught in an open field with a storm approaching. Since entering Carmel in 1969, she had gone out for dentist's and doctor's appointments, but otherwise had spent the last twenty-eight years in a world without television, radios, newspapers, movies, fashion, or men.

She approached the car and greeted Sister Mary Michael, the community's extern nun, who wore the full habit but had not taken the same vows of claustration as the others. Sister Mary Michael lived in a small building outside the enclosure where her duties included maintaining the external chapel, greeting parishioners, and shopping for the community. She attended Mass every day, separated from the cloistered nuns by a screen, but was otherwise free to create her own balance of prayer and work.

"You'll have to roll down your window—it gets awfully hot," Sister Mary Michael explained over the roar of the heater. "Mr. Yoshinobu taught me to do this, it draws the heat away from the engine. The radiator is very tired, poor thing." The community's 1974 Plymouth Valiant had traveled nearly two hundred thousand miles, all on its original engine. The mechanic who facilitated this ongoing miracle, Mr. Yoshinobu, had earned a permanent spot on the nuns' prayer list.

Sister John kept her eyes on the rearview mirror and watched as the monastery got smaller. When the driveway rounded a bend, the compound disappeared behind a stand of eucalyptus trees. After another bend, the car reached the street leading down toward the Golden State Freeway, and Sister John had to remind herself of God's presence as the Plymouth merged into traffic. In less than five minutes she had traveled from a world where the present was eternal to a place where the present moment did not seem to exist at all. People in their cars, the cars themselves, the buildings, the signs—even the sky, which was turned into a thoroughfare by all of the air traffic—looked squeezed up against an infinitesimal future, like a crowd trying to escape a burning building through a pinhole. Sister Mary Michael exited less than a mile from where they had gotten onto the concrete river, parked the Miracle, then the two Carmelites began walking.

From the outside, County Hospital looked like a cross between a Masonic lodge and the Tower of Babel, with inscriptions in foreign languages carved all over its stone façade. The stairs leading up to it seemed to go on forever, blinding the two nuns with reflected sunlight. When they stepped inside the lobby, it took their eyes a few moments to adjust to the darkness. Sister Mary Michael approached the information booth and asked a man sitting behind a bulletproof window for directions to the neurology department.

"Fifth floor."

Sister Mary Michael smiled at him. "And where might one find the elevator?"

He pointed without smiling back.

They got into a crowded elevator where a middle-aged Hispanic man, seeing the two Carmelites, removed his hat and greeted them in Spanish. The others in the elevator seemed uncomfortable around the nuns, and averted their eyes. When the Sisters got off the elevator at the fifth floor and took their places in line at the reception desk, several patients in the waiting area stared openly.

Sister John kept custody of her eyes, letting her gaze settle on the floor in front of her. She did not need to see the faces to feel the mixture of curiosity, amusement, and hostility directed toward her. This was why so many nuns in the nursing and teaching orders had chosen to abandon the traditional habit. In the cloister, the habit eliminated distractions; out here, it created them. Sister John considered the irony: the habit was originally adopted by nuns to make them inconspicuous *in* the world. In the Middle Ages, a plain serge tunic, linen wimple, and veil was the outfit favored by poor widows. A true habit now, Sister John thought as she glanced around the waiting room, would be a nylon jogging outfit worn over tennis shoes.

The nuns sat down under a television set tuned to a daytime talk show.

Nothing must be rejected, nothing must be despised. It is all God.

The subject of the program was paternity; a man had accused his wife of infidelity and suspected that the child she was bearing was not his own. She denied the accusations and had agreed to a blood test, the results of which were to be announced at the end of the program. Nuns and monks accustomed to silence tend to become skilled at reading faces; it was immediately clear to Sister John that the host and the studio audience, although expressing verbal support for the accused woman, were hoping she would be proved a liar. No mention was made of the unborn child, or its future.

Sister John looked away from the television, not wanting to learn the results of the test. She stared up at the ceiling and let her thoughts wander away from the hospital.

The ceiling in the attic bedroom slanted in one direction, following the line of the roof. The asymmetry of it nauseated her if she stared up at it for too long.

The window faced east. In the mornings she lay in bed and watched specks of dust flash into being, drift without reaching anywhere, then blink off. If she watched long enough, she could make herself forget about the beam of sunlight and imagine that the specks appeared and disappeared on their own. Did God make them? She would savor that mystery until it began to lose flavor, then have the thrill of remembering that something silent and invisible streamed through the window and breathed fire into anything that crossed its path. Was that God? Switching perspectives like that kept the mystery fresh.

During the summer, locusts went off like broken alarms in the trees. One of them had shed its skin on the branch just outside her window. The hollow shell clung to the bark for weeks, as if waiting for its owner to return, then disappeared during a thunderstorm. Helen found it the next morning, soggy and missing several legs, in a bunch of leaves caught in a storm drain.

The front screen door wheezed open, then shut. Footsteps crossed the kitchen, then stopped at the base of the stairs.

"A letter from your mom, Helen."

The little girl skied down the stairs, socks polishing the steps, took the envelope from her grandmother, then returned to her attic bedroom. She lay on her stomach on the bed and used a pencil as a letter opener. She looked at the folded paper inside and made herself wait a few seconds before pulling it out.

She read it straight through and got angry with herself for not making it last longer. Then she became angry at her mother. The letter was only a page in length, told her nothing, and ended the way they all did: "Write soon!" Helen always wrote soon, then waited months for a response.

She put the letter in the drawer where she kept all of her mother's letters, under her balled-up socks. The screen door wheezed again and her grandmother started beating the dirt out of a rug with a broom. Housework and locusts: theme music for summer tedium. Helen shut the window, wrapped a pillow around her head, and rocked until she went numb.

"Sister John?"

A nurse with a clipboard stood a few yards away.

"The doctor is ready for you. Would you follow me?"

The nurse walked with an athlete's confidence. Her movements painted a bright rainbow through time. Sister John, by contrast, walked as if hoping to become invisible. She wanted to leave a different sort of trail behind her, a wake of serenity. She hoped it might pull others toward God without their being aware of it.

The nurse led her to a small room. Seeing that the sheet of paper covering the examination table was wrinkled, the nurse tugged at it until fresh paper spun out of the roll and covered the table. She tore off the used part—the noise made Sister John flinch—and invited the nun to sit down. The paper crackled disagreeably under Sister John's weight.

Checking over the admission sheet, the nurse asked, "You're here to see the doctor about headaches?"

"Yes."

The nurse had a cotton hospital gown tucked under her arm, but, after a glance at Sister John, decided it wouldn't be necessary. "The doctor will be in to see you shortly," she said, leaving the room and closing the door behind her.

Alone in a space that was about the same size as her cell, Sister John found herself staring at a large plastic model of the human brain and spinal cord. The brain had been partly disassembled to reveal its white inner structure, while the major nerves had been painted red and blue. It looked like a mad scientist's attempt to explain patriotism. Everything in the room was designed for either measurement or analysis. Scales, thermometers, charts, probes, diagnostic manuals, tongue depressors, reflex hammers. The sterile paper on the bed was a reminder that this was not a place to rest or heal;

your unclean body was to lie on it only as long as it took to examine you.

Yet it was God's room all the same. The door opened and a man in a white lab coat stepped halfway inside, then paused to give instructions to someone down the hall.

Your will, not mine.

The doctor lowered a stack of files and a ceramic mug onto the counter and picked up the clipboard the nurse had left for him. He studied the admission sheet as if unaware that his patient was in the room. This gave Sister John an opportunity to adjust to the fact that her doctor looked young enough to be her son.

He finished reading the sheet, sat down on a stool, and looked at her for the first time. His expression chilled her; she felt as if she were being watched from behind a one-way mirror.

"I'm Dr. Sheppard. How are you today?"

"Very well, thank you."

"Tell me about your headaches."

The smell of coffee reminded her to dwell in the moment, in God's present. In the convent, they brewed their coffee weak as a matter of economy. Whatever the doctor had in his mug, she guessed from the fragrance, must have used a lot of grounds.

The paper under her crackled again when she began to speak.

"They started around three years ago. When I saw my regular doctor about them, he told me they were migraines, and that there wasn't much to do about them except learn to work around them. I'm fine with that—it's my prioress who's concerned. She was a nurse once, so she's especially cautious when it comes to health." After the incident during recreation, when Sister John had not responded to questions for several seconds after dropping her notebook, Mother Emmanuel had insisted on a visit to a specialist.

"Did your regular doctor run any tests for you?"

"No, but if anything was seriously wrong with me, I think he would know it. I've been seeing him for almost twenty years."

Dr. Sheppard began taking notes. "How often do you get the headaches?"

"Sometimes twice a month, sometimes every other day. They seem to come in cycles."

"Do they ever wake you up at night? Out of a sound sleep?"

"Not that I can recall."

The doctor finished his coffee, then began the standard neurological exam by asking her what day and year it was and to name the current president. When she answered those questions without difficulty, he asked her to remove her sandals. Lowering himself to one knee, he cradled one of her feet in the palm of his hand and drew a cotton swab across the sole and over her toes, testing for sensation and reflexes. He did the same with the point of a safety pin, using it so skillfully that it neither hurt nor tickled.

During this procedure, Sister John thought of Mother Mary Joseph, who, every year on Holy Thursday, used to kneel down in imitation of Christ to wash the feet of all the nuns. She pictured the doctor kneeling before patients every day, holding their feet and listening to their complaints and struggling to cure their diseases. How could she have taken so long to welcome the Christ in him?

Each time I forget You, I add to your suffering.

He washed his hands as she put her sandals back on and asked, "Do you notice anything else around the time of these headaches? Funny things happening to your vision, say, or a sense of altered consciousness?" When she hesitated, the doctor's face showed interest. "Even if it's something trivial, like smelling broccoli or hearing advertising jingles," he added.

How, she wondered, do you talk about infused contemplation with a neurologist? She took a breath to center herself, then said, "I try to see the pain as an opportunity, not an affliction. If I surrender to it in the right way, I have the feeling of transcending my body completely. It's a wonderful experience, but it's spiritual, not physical."

Without looking up from his note-taking, the doctor asked, "Do you keep a journal?"

"I do write every day, yes. Mostly poetry." She resisted the temptation to tell him she'd had a book published.

"Do you fill notebooks quickly?"

This question took her by surprise, even more than the one about altered consciousness. "I suppose I do. Is that bad?"

"Not necessarily—it's a standard question." He took an envelope-sized form out of a drawer and began filling it in, then pulled a pink copy out from under the top sheet. "Migraine is still a likely explanation for your symptoms, but there are a few other possibilities I'd like to rule out before we start discussing ways to manage the pain." He handed her the pink sheet. "On your way out, give this to the nurse at the station where you checked in. I've written you up for an EEG and a CT scan. They're painless, safe tests, and the nurse can schedule them for the same day. As soon as I've gotten the results, I'll call you and we'll go from there."

Sister John looked at the cutaway model of the brain and decided not to ask about the other possibilities.

God is as present in illness as He is in health—maybe even more so. All that matters is that we accept what is offered, and trust in Him completely.

When the doctor stood up to leave, she forced a smile. "Peace be with you, Doctor." She was so used to the exchange of blessings that when he answered with only, "Have a great day," she felt the absence. She could no longer remember what it felt like to live apart from God, to act without an awareness of God.

How blessed I am to know that God is real. What a gift, to know that God's love never fails.

Twelfth Sunday in Ordinary Time

Desert poppies opened toward the sun.

A glimmer just outside the scriptorium window caught Sister John's attention. A dewdrop caught in a spider's web flashed like a prism.

We hang suspended in His love.

Ink glistened on paper, following the tip of her pen, then sank flat.

When one heart moves, the whole web trembles.

Her tests had been scheduled for the following week. Until then, she could only wait and pray that whatever the results were, she would still be allowed to go to the Vatican in October. She had begun a novena to Saint Thérèse asking for help, and already the saint had given her a favorable sign: a dream in which she saw herself dressed in white, lying on a white bed in a white room. Since white was the liturgical color for both Christmas and Easter, she interpreted the dream to mean that a cycle would soon be completed.

> *The weaver stays hidden.*

She stopped writing, sensing that she was being watched. Torn for a moment between worlds; it hurt to lift her eyes. Sister Miriam stood in the doorway, holding a breakfast tray. "Mother Emmanuel said you hadn't taken any breakfast," she blurted, embarrassed to have been caught staring. "She asked me to bring something to you."

The novice had toasted a muffin and spread it with butter and homemade kumquat jam, prepared a cup of coffee, and even tucked a jasmine blossom into the napkin holder.

When Sister John thanked her for the kindness, the novice bowed in response, as if to say: I do this for God.

"Will you join me, Sister Miriam?"

She looked flustered. "I've already eaten, thank you."

"Stay for a few minutes anyway. I'd like to know how you're doing."

The white veil bobbed dutifully. Sister John put the jasmine blossom on a sheet of vellum and tucked the napkin under her chin. "I remember feeling excited about making first vows," she said, "but also nervous. The professed Sisters all seemed so *complete* to me, whereas I still felt like something that had been pulled out of the oven early."

Sister Miriam kept her eyes on the table. "I'm grateful to God for the opportunity. I hope I can become worthy of the honor."

"You already are, Sister."

Sister Miriam glanced up at Sister John. The manner was submissive, but the look in the eyes was not. "May I ask a personal question?"

"Of course."

"How did your family feel about your vocation?"

Sister John couldn't remember the last time anyone had asked her that. It didn't seem like a personal question at all; her former life seemed so far away that answering it was like talking about someone else.

"I was raised by my grandparents. My grandfather had gone to God by the time I entered, and my grandmother was already quite ill. When I told her my decision, she asked if monasteries had washing machines. I think that might have been our only conversation about it."

The novice had a way of appearing both peaceful and uncomfortable at the same time. True serenity looks spontaneous, but Sister Miriam's looked intentional.

"My parents don't think I belong here," she said.

"Still?"

The novice shook her head. "I'm worried that it's going to be even worse when they see me in the habit."

"Are they coming out for your ceremony?"

Sister Miriam ran her fingers over a piece of vellum on her side of the Ark. "No, but they're coming next week. To try to talk me out of it."

"I'm so sorry . . . If you'll give me their names, I'll put them on my prayer list right away."

Sister Miriam wrote the names on a slip of paper, then stood up. "If there is any other way that I can be of service to you, please don't hesitate to ask. Praised be Jesus Christ."

"May He be forever praised."

Sister Miriam bowed, then faded from the room.

All of us will be tested in faith, again and again.

Sister Angelica's canaries began singing from their cage under the eaves. They were like flowers made of sound, a perfect accompaniment to the visual splendor of the garden. But the cage—it reminded Sister John of her years of emptiness, when she felt trapped in the cloister. And even before that, of the Saturday mornings when her grandfather used to drive her out to the poultry farm in Steubenville to get fresh eggs.

The cages at the farm were stacked in rows, four high and thirty down, over long pits overflowing with excrement. All this in a corrugated metal warehouse that felt like a refrigerator in winter and an oven in summer. The cages were so small the chickens couldn't stand up, and since they were never released for exercise, their nails grew long and curved around the bars underneath them.

Between the overpowering smell and the sight of all that miserable confinement, Helen preferred to wait outside in the dirt lot next to the warehouse. She searched for dirt bombs—clods of dry earth, suitable for throwing—and sent them whistling against the cinderblock foundation of the shed. These exploded with a satisfying noise and cloud of dust, and left a cone of red dirt at the point of impact.

She would daydream about sneaking into the warehouse at night and releasing the chickens, then visiting their colony years later and finding that she had become a legend over the course of several avian generations. In these daydreams she did not reveal herself as the savior from the distant past, but asked questions about the Great Escape, and thrilled to hear the chickens describe her as a radiant goddess.

Her grandfather stopped to fill his truck at the Sinclair station and buy a bag of potato chips. The attendant, an old bachelor with a turkey neck, whistled out of key as he turned the crank to the gas pump.

When the truck got rolling again, the bleached concrete highway turned into a gray river, and the stain from all the spilled oil and exhaust in the center of the lane turned into a dark serpent just under the surface. Her grandfather wouldn't turn on the radio because all the local stations carried evangelist revivals on Sunday, and he couldn't abide their shouting and the way they faced their congregations during services, turning their backs on God. He didn't talk as he drove, either. The sound of the engine and of the tires singing over the pavement seemed to hypnotize him.

She noticed he was not slowing down for the exit at Johnson's silo. When they drove right past it, Helen's heart raced. Part of her knew that he had just gotten distracted, but another part fantasized that they were setting off to find her mother.

He realized his mistake after only a few seconds, eased over onto the shoulder, and made a U-turn.

"What's the matter with you?" he asked when he saw she was crying.

"I'm sick of going to that egg place. It stinks there."

He looked puzzled. Rows of young corn whizzed by on one side of the road, and newly plowed fields stretched off to the horizon on the other. He rolled down the window and the smell of manure rushed into the car.

"It stinks everywhere, honey. Just tell yourself it's sweet. And if that doesn't work, you can always breathe through your mouth."

Gregory the Great, Pope and Doctor

The odor of disinfectant mortified Sister John's sense of smell. A scheduling nurse had instructed her to sleep less than four hours the night before her tests. As she wandered through the hospital on her way to the testing area, she felt like a bird that had flown into a giant factory and couldn't find its way out. She tried following the signs on the wall, but eventually had to ask a policeman for directions. His arms were folded across his chest, with his fists tucked under the biceps to make them look bigger. His gun looked like a steel wasp, the bullets deadly larvae. When he pointed their location out on a photocopied map, Sister John noticed that he kept his thumbs tucked out of sight. When he crossed his arms again, she caught a glimpse of one, and saw that the nail and cuticle were badly chewed. He suddenly looked like a boy dressed up as a policeman.

Even with the delay of getting lost in the hospital, she checked in at the EEG room an hour early. She sat down in the waiting room and stayed awake with the help of the rosary, but when she'd finished the cycle, her mind wandered. She drifted in the present, knowing that she was in a hospital, but it seemed like a dollhouse version of a hospital, and she felt like a dollhouse version of a patient. It was like a dream.

"We're ready for you now, Sister."

The nurse-technician, a small woman with shiny, jet-black hair, wearing a crisply starched uniform, led her into the testing room. "If you'll take off your veil and lie down on that bed, I'll set up the equipment for you."

"What does it do?" Sister John asked.

"It measures the electrical activity in your brain. Don't worry, you can't feel anything at all. All we want you to do is try to relax and fall asleep." When Sister John took off her veil, the nurse saw that her head was shaved and said, "Perfect! Makes my job much easier. How long have you been a nun now?"

"Almost thirty years."

"Long time! I went to Catholic school in Manila." She laughed as she said this. "Those nuns were strict! One got mad at me for winning a cha-cha contest and made me stand bent over, holding my ankles, until I fell down." She tapped the side of her head with her finger. "That lady had problems, I think." After a final check of the equipment, the technician turned off the lights in the room.

"Just try to sleep. I'll wake you up when it's done."

Sister John closed her eyes and imagined confronting this overzealous nun in the Chapter of Faults, where the habit symbolized obedience rather than authority, and where even a Superior could be criticized for her human failings. Remembering that the technician had asked her to try to sleep, however, she let go of her anger and began praying the rosary again. She coordinated her breathing with the phrases, an exercise she had learned as a postulant to calm her mind, and barely reached the second Joyful Mystery before nodding off.

For the CT scan, she had to change into a white hospital gown and remove even her crucifix and wedding band, symbol of her mystical marriage. When she stepped into the testing room and saw that the walls, floor, and machinery were all white, she was overwhelmed by a sense of having seen it before, of having been in that very room. A nurse helped her lie down on a pallet with her head clamped inside a great white circle. The room even sounded white, smelled white.

She remembered the novena to Saint Thérèse, and the dream. What cycle was being completed here?

I will not struggle against You, no matter where You lead me.

The machine made a clicking noise as the scanner shot beams of radiation through her skull. Each picture would represent a slice, eight millimeters thick, of her brain. She surrendered to it and reminded herself that none of this was an accident. God planned everything down to the smallest details, and everything He did had a positive meaning and coherence.

From all around and within her, His presence shook like thunder, until all other sensation was drowned out.

Perfect affirmation, perfect understanding, perfect silence: Your love, dear God, in full voice.

Twelfth Thursday in Ordinary Time

Toward the end of summer, families of deer began wandering down to the cloister from the parched hills, attracted by the scent of the garden. Unable to get into the enclosure, they had to settle for the ivy growing on the outer walls.

Sister John listened to them from her darkened cell. Every so often a doe would call to its fawns with a plaintive murmur; their footfalls answered her.

> *As the deer longs for running streams,*
> *so my soul longs for you, O God.*

Forbidden to write at night, she could only watch as the poetry of liturgy merged with the poetry of memory, flowing past but leaving no trace.

Heat rose from the pavement at night. The trees sighed overhead.

She rounded a bend, out of range of the last streetlight. She saw her breath in the moonlight, pausing at the foot of her driveway. She could see into the brightly lit house, but was herself invisible. This is what spies must feel like, she thought.

Usually, at this time of the evening, her grandfather would be reading the paper in the living room. She guessed he was in the shed, fixing something. After a few minutes of staring into the empty house, the darkness spooked her and drove her inside. She threw her jacket on the sofa and announced her return, but got no response. She walked into the kitchen and her body went rigid. String beans scattered all over the floor, an overturned colander, and a scrawled note on the kitchen table.

Hushed voices, too-long hugs, the cheerless confetti of flowers and sympathy cards.

The sound of high heels on wood floors. Cars parked all the way to the end of the driveway and out into the street. Casserole pots and lasagna trays, the smell of perfume.

The drapes at the funeral parlor were slightly frayed where they brushed against the carpet. Her grandfather's hands were folded in front of him, but when she looked closely, she saw they weren't actually resting against his body. They hovered slightly above, spoiling the illusion. How peaceful can you be when you're stiff? During the slow-motion car ride from the church to the cemetery, her grandmother—who had barely spoken for days—looked at Helen's long brown hair, reached out to stroke it, then said, "You've got much nicer hair than your mother. Hers always looked so stringy."

The call finally came, two weeks later. It was the first time Helen had heard her mother's voice in ten years. She was obviously drunk, and offered no apology for missing the funeral. Their conversation faltered, each trying to avoid being the first to say anything of substance. "How's Grandma taking it?" she finally asked.

Helen wanted to yell at her, to hurt her in some way, but she did not. "Not very well. You want to talk to her?"

A pause. "Yes."

Helen called upstairs, "It's my mother on the phone. She says she just got the letter."

The old woman came downstairs, walked into the kitchen, took the phone from Helen, and hung it up without a word.

Helen stayed in the kitchen for a long time, trying not to stare at the phone. Her mother never called back.

Twelfth Friday
in Ordinary Time

"Did you say 'fire'?" Sister Teresa asked. The invalid nun stared straight ahead, her cheeks sunken.

"No, Sister, I asked if you wanted any more pie."

"Who's going to die?"

"No one's going to die. Everything's fine, and you're having dinner now. Here—have another bite."

"Who are you?"

"I'm Sister John of the Cross. And look who this is." Sister John pointed to one of the photographs on the bureau, placed there in hopes of stimulating the elderly woman's memory. The picture was taken on Sister Teresa's twenty-first birthday, just before she entered Carmel.

"Can you tell me who it is?"

Sister Teresa showed no sign of recognizing herself, but the crisis had been averted. "Can I go home now?"

"This is home, Sister. We're in the Carmel of St. Joseph. God is all around us."

Sister Teresa frowned. "I don't want any caramel, I want to go home."

The sounds of conversation drifted in through the infirmary window. Sister John looked out and saw Sister Elizabeth and Sister Christine chatting near the fountain, tossing pieces of bread into the fountain for the birds. Reflected sunlight and crosshatched shadows danced across Saint Joseph's robes.

The window curtains billowed. Sister Anne entered the infirmary with a bucket in one hand and a mop in the other, getting right to work without even nodding a greeting. Sister Anne was a declared Soul of Penance, someone who felt a special calling to make reparations on behalf of those either unwilling or unable to do it for themselves. She rarely spoke about the mystical life of Carmel, feeling that it was presumptuous to expect God to grant supernatural favors. Obedience to the monastic rule, she believed, was the only sure means of pleasing God. Anything beyond that was a matter of grace, and for God only to decide.

The muscles in her forearms quivered as she put the weight of her upper body into each stroke of the mop. Unable to sit still while the seventy-eight-year-old nun cleaned the floor, Sister John approached. "Please, let me help you, Sister. I can—"

The interruption was crisp. "You can help by getting more

rest. Your health is important to God, even if it's not important to you."

Sister John knew better than to try to argue. She fed the rest of the pie to Sister Teresa, then combed the elderly nun's snowy hair. "You look nice today, Sister."

A look of confusion. "You're not my sister." Sister Teresa looked down at her nightgown and started picking at it.

Someday this will be me. Will I be ready?

Sister John looked out toward the garden, where Sister Miriam had just fastened one corner of a sheet to the line with a clothespin and was about to pin the other when the bell rang for Sext. Taking the principle of obedience to an extreme, the novice let the unfastened corner drop to the ground and immediately began walking to choir.

Sister John thought of the regimentation of bells and periods in school, the sense of being shoved from one place to another, of being kept quiet and under control, of being broken like horses. Here in the monastery, she and the others submitted willingly to a regimentation far stricter, but with entirely different results.

We free ourselves for God. Here, we are liberated from the tyranny of the self.

Birth of Mary

Before leaving the monastery to hear the results of her tests, Sister John lit a votive candle in memory of Saint Gertrude, a Benedictine mystic who spent nearly as much of her cloistered life in the infirmary as in choir. When God asked Saint Gertrude if she wished for better physical health, she answered: *I desire nothing but Thy holy will.* By suffering in union with the crucified Christ, she turned the ravages of illness into the ravishment of surrender, and became both more human and more holy.

This time, when Sister John reached the hospital and took her seat in the examination room, she felt ready. The pieces of equipment around her posed no threat. They were no different from spoons or fountain pens or lawn rakes. The sounds of the hospital no longer seemed dissonant; her ears had merely needed time to awaken to God's rich counterpoint.

Dr. Sheppard stepped in, greeted her, then opened her file across his knees. As he turned the pages, a pamphlet slid out of the file and onto the floor. The cover showed two healthy-looking people smiling at each other. Under that image, Sister John saw the title: *Living with Epilepsy.*

She felt the blood rush out of her face and limbs toward her heart, protecting it from the sudden chill. Sister John had come prepared to hear bad news about her health, but not about the state of her soul. She knew quite well that one of the first questions asked of anyone wishing to become a cloistered nun was, "Have you ever been treated for mental illness or epilepsy?" If the answer was yes to either, the candidate was automatically rejected. Epilepsy was particularly feared because of its reputation for producing compelling—but false—visions. Doctors and clergy alike had referred to the disease for centuries as "holy madness."

Please, God, take anything, take my life

The doctor picked the brochure up without comment, and put it back into the file. "The results of your tests are back," he said, "and while it might not sound like good news, I think you'll see that it's not so bad, either."

but don't take Yourself away from me, don't tell me I haven't known You at all

"The EEG showed that you have an epileptic disorder, but so far the seizure activity is localized in the temporal-lobe area of the brain. That's good—it's kept you from having any grand-mal attacks, the kind that spread across the brain and cause convulsions. Temporal-lobe seizures tend to be more psychological."

I waited for so long, Lord

"The symptoms vary, which is why it's difficult to diagnose without the tests. Some patients experience their seizures as attacks of nostalgia or déjà vu, while others find that their senses are heightened. I had one patient who became convinced that she could 'read' people's moods by their smell alone. Unfortunately, she found this ability so thrilling she couldn't resist sniffing whoever happened to be around her, and she worked as a museum guard. That's one of the characteristics of the disorder, by the way—becoming so drawn into the altered world created by the disorder that one loses interest in everything else."

He delivered this information in a brisk, matter-of-fact tone, as if talking about a third person who was not in the room.

"But now the good news. The CT scan found what's causing the seizures, and we can do something about it. You have a small meningioma—about the size of a raisin—just above your right ear. It's in an excellent position for removal, just under the skull. I've consulted with a surgeon about it, and he said they should be able to peel it right off. It'll be a very clean procedure, very straightforward. If we take care of it now, while the seizures are still localized, your prognosis for complete recovery is excellent."

Even with the doctor sitting with his knees almost touching hers, she felt more alone than she ever had in her cell. Still, she knew that the real test of faith came when one faced a situation for which there was no human answer.

He sifted through the file and removed some papers, including the pamphlet that had fallen out earlier. "These materials answer most of the questions patients have when they are first diagnosed. If there's anything you don't understand, or if you just want to talk more about it, feel free to call me anytime. I just want to repeat that the news is positive. Once we've removed that tumor, I predict you'll be as good as new."

She stared down at her hands. The artificial light of the hospital made her wedding band look dull.

God made me as I am. Each of us is given a unique cross to bear, each situation in life a personal call to become holy. He would not have taken me on this journey for nothing.

1969

The Call

Triumph of the Cross

The driver carried her suitcase to the door, then refused to let her pay him for the ride. "My treat," he said, looking up at the wall surrounding the convent. "You may need the money for the fare back if you change your mind."

"I won't change my mind," Helen said.

He shook his head. "Good luck, then."

As the cab pulled away, she took one last look at a world that seemed committed to destroying itself, then turned her back on it.

I'm ready.

The bell in the campanile tower rang three times. When the last note died away, a voice called from the other side of the door:

"What do you ask?"

Helen called back, "To love God with all my heart."

The door opened slowly. A nun whose veil covered her face beckoned Helen inside.

She took a deep breath and stepped through, saying to herself as she crossed the border between worlds,

There's no turning back. The person I was no longer exists.

The veiled nun leaned forward and whispered, "Don't forget your things, dear." Helen had to step back outside to get her suitcase.

Once she was inside for good, the nun closed and bolted the door, handed her a crucifix, and delivered the prioress's blessing for new arrivals: *Passio Christi, conforta me.* Helen knelt down to kiss the crucifix, then hung it around her neck.

At last the nun pulled her veil back. "I am Mother Mary Joseph." To Helen's disappointment, the prioress looked like a woman she knew in Ohio who organized 4-H bake sales. The resemblance faded when the prioress smiled, however; her eyes were as clear and peaceful as a dove's. "Welcome to Carmel, Sister Helen. May you find God here."

Sister Helen. Her new name in religion would come after a year's service to God, but for now, just to be referred to as "Sister" felt like a radical transformation.

Mother Mary Joseph led her to the choir, where they knelt

together before the Blessed Sacrament. "Take a few minutes to let God know what is in your heart right now," she whispered.

Please, God, let me know You.

After that, the prioress led her into the whitewashed corridor facing the garden. "We prayed that you would join us, Sister. Now that you have become a part of our community, remember to pray for *us*. Pray that we all remember we are here for one reason only: to please God."

A second nun appeared in the hallway and bowed to the new arrival.

"I am Sister Teresa, your novice mistress. I wish you God's peace." She picked up Helen's suitcase and said, "Follow me, please."

She led Helen up a short flight of stairs to the dormitory, where she paused in front of a closed door. "This cell is your crucible, the pillar of cloud where God spoke to Moses. It must never become just another room." She opened the door.

The room contained a bed, a cross, a chair, and a desk.

"Nothing but God," Sister Teresa whispered.

Her postulant's outfit—a simple brown dress, cape, and short veil—was laid out on the bed. Sister Teresa handed her the suitcase. "A nun's cell is for her and God alone. No other Sister may enter it without permission. I'll come back in an hour to take you to the garden for your reception ceremony. The others are all looking forward to meeting you."

Helen stepped into her cell, and the door closed behind her. It took her only a few minutes to change into the brown dress and cape. She put her old clothes into her suitcase and slid it under the bed, out of sight.

My crucible.

She had never heard silence like it; she had expected the sound of fullness, but it sounded like absolute nothingness instead.

Nothing but God.

After only a few minutes of sitting in the chair, she became restless. She thought of lying down on the bed to relax, but immediately chastised herself.

I didn't come all this way to be comfortable, I came here to work. Now it begins: I will think only of God.

She faced the white wall and tried to meditate, but saw mirages in the stucco: ridges, swirls, pools, plains. Torsos, hands, eyes. Shapes that defied interpretation, yet filled her with apprehension.

She closed her eyes and tried to empty her mind of all that

was not God, but found that it was like trying to empty an ocean: where do you put the water?

They had magic pockets.

It seemed that the nuns at St. Ina's Catholic School could produce anything from the folds of their ample garments: keys, pencils, tissues, chalk, erasers, prayer books, gold stars with adhesive on the back, and even treats for children who had been especially good. Their habits were like houses; Helen imagined that they slept standing up in church, their hands tucked in their sleeves and their veils billowing out like tents.

The nuns taught the children that there were as many ways to love God as there were Christian souls, but vocations to the religious life were especially pleasing to the Lord. By the second grade, every girl had asked God for the grace of a vocation to become a nun, and every boy had announced a calling to the priesthood. One had even turned his basement into a seminary and used old beach towels for practice vestments.

Helen collected holy cards, made her own reliquaries, and marveled at the lives of the saints, especially those who had managed to keep the faith as they were being torn to pieces, boiled, or burned. During actual church services and Sunday school, however, her mind wandered. The miracle of God's presence in everyday life simply could not compete with the stupendous events of the past—until she met Sister Priscilla.

While Helen was in the seventh grade, one of the Sisters vanished. One day Sister Beatrice was teaching music and English and American history; the next day she was gone. No explanation for her disappearance was offered to the students, and any mention of her name was met with blank stares, as if she had never existed. Her replacement, Sister Priscilla, showed up a week later.

At first Helen disliked the new teacher. She assigned more homework than the other nuns, and in her gym class she actually made the girls exercise rather than letting them play hopscotch or jump rope. One day she instructed the girls to run once around the school to warm up. As soon as Helen and her classmates rounded the first corner of the building, the teasing began.

"Look at the way she runs!"

"Watch out—if she falls on you, you're dead!"

Helen stopped running and walked the rest of the way. She pretended to ignore the way Eleanor Peters imitated her by splaying her feet and waddling, but as soon as the others were out of sight, she tried forcing her thighs closer together. It only made her fatty's gait worse. When she rounded the last bend and appeared from behind the building, Sister Priscilla looked agitated.

"Why did you stop running, Miss Nye?"

"I'm no good at it."

A few of the girls snickered, but Sister Priscilla cut them down with a look. "You think it's funny? None of you are good at it, either."

Helen's face burned. The new teacher was only making matters worse.

Sister Priscilla removed her glasses and let them hang around her neck from a chain. "None of us is good at anything without God's help. And God only helps those who make an effort. Do you want God's help, Miss Nye?"

Helen looked down at her shoes. Dew had soaked them through, and the toes were streaked with grass stains. She wished there was some way to escape, somewhere to escape to, someone to become.

"Yes Sister."

"I want you to run around the school again, this time by yourself. This time I want you to show God what you're capable of."

Completely humiliated in front of the others, she jogged off, rounded the corner, then collapsed against the damp brick wall. She cried herself out, then started walking again. It didn't matter now; she was going to be yelled at, no matter what she did. The school-yard sloped off toward a marsh grown thick with cattails. She watched a blackbird fly straight into the reeds without touching any of them, an onyx needle threading an ocher loom.

If I could fly like that bird, she thought, I'd poke everybody's eyes out and get away with it.

Guilt over this evil thought rose up and knocked her loose. She went into a flat-footed, arm-flailing sprint. Her shoes slapped the ground and the soles of her feet ached, but she kept it up past the kindergarteners' swing set, past the monkey bars, around the chapel, and down the hill on the other side of the school. Her lungs felt as if they would tear open. All of the strength drained out of her chubby legs and she thought she might topple forward, face-first into the grass. She knew she looked ridiculous as she came around the last corner, but was too frenzied by now to care. She came to a floppy halt in front of Sister Priscilla, gasped for breath, then dropped to her knees and threw up.

Sister Priscilla helped her to a stoop near the door to the school auditorium and rubbed her shoulders. "My goodness! You've got to pace yourself, don't you know that?"

Helen felt too dizzy to speak.

The nun said nothing for a long time. "I underestimated you, Miss Nye. I won't make that mistake again."

She pulled a tissue out of the pocket in her sleeve so that Helen could wipe her mouth.

"I may need a student to help me with certain extra duties—a monitor, someone I know I can count on to do her best. Would you be interested?"

Helen nodded. She felt encouraged, but at the same time wondered why it was that grownups, who were usually so averse to foolishness in children, sometimes turned around and treated it like a virtue.

Sister Priscilla soon became Helen's model for a fully realized human being; in fact, she seemed superhuman. While most nuns looked like museum guards in their habits, protecting something that had been vital long ago, Sister Priscilla looked like vitality itself. On her, the veil spoke of mastery rather than sacrifice, of living mystery rather than dead tradition. When she looked at Helen, Helen felt as if a powerful light had been trained on her—the sort of light a jeweler might use while cutting and polishing a diamond.

Time seemed at Sister Priscilla's disposal. While Helen experienced time as the measurement of waiting—waiting for her mother to return, waiting for her life to begin—for Sister Priscilla, all the waiting seemed to be over. The main event was under way; time was a measurement of action.

And her actions were all beautiful. She turned even the most ordinary tasks, like pulling maps down or emptying the pencil sharpener, into sacraments. On the other hand, she could talk about faith in a way that made it sound like common sense. She made divine things seem human, and human things seem divine.

"When I was thirteen," Sister Priscilla told the class after their weekly atomic bomb drill, "my parents asked me what I wanted for Christmas. I said that I wanted to go to Italy. In Sunday school we had just learned about the Christian martyrs, and more than anything in the world, I wanted to see the Colosseum where they had died. It was childish curiosity, but I was persistent. For months I pestered them about it, just to show them I was serious. In the process, I became interested in much more than just the Colosseum."

She crossed the room and stood in profile against the blinds, her silhouette all clean lines and angles.

"On Christmas morning I was sure I would find a boat ticket under the tree, but instead I received an Italian language primer. I was heartbroken, but my mother forced me to give it a try and I ended up taking lessons from a tutor. I finally did get to go to Italy, years later, and had experiences there I could never have had without being able to speak the language."

She turned to face the class.

"From my childish point of view, the book seemed a disappointing gift. From where I stand now, I see that it was a wise, loving choice. What can this teach us about suffering, do you think?"

A fly on the windowsill suddenly came to life, spinning on its back and buzzing loudly. None of the students raised their hands to answer the question.

"I'll change the question slightly. We are told that God only allows to happen to us what is for our own good, but what about when bad things happen? How could that possibly be for our good?"

The fly bounced across the edge of the sill and fell into a heating vent, and the buzzing stopped.

"I can't answer those questions for you," Sister Priscilla finally said, looking right at Helen. "No human person can. But we can all think about this: compared to the One who created the universe, we are all *children. Just because we cannot understand what happens to us doesn't mean that God doesn't."*

A knock at her cell door.

"Praised be Jesus Christ."

"Come in."

Sister Teresa opened the door, but stayed outside. "When someone says, 'Praised be Jesus Christ,' you must answer, 'May He be forever praised.' That is how we greet each other." She smiled, then asked, "How does the dress feel?"

"A little tight, but I can let it out. I brought a sewing kit."

"Don't let it out too much; today is the first day of the Fast of the Order, which lasts until Easter. We all start losing weight now."

The cloister bell rang twice.

"That's for you. Follow me to the garden, Sister."

Helen blushed, and Sister Teresa seemed to read her thoughts. "In the beginning, we all feel a bit like impostors in our capes and veils and being called 'Sister.' But don't worry about it—just act like you think a nun should when you're not sure what to do, and you'll find that through grace and love, you become one."

The eighteen Sisters of the Carmel of St. Joseph stood waiting in a half-circle in the garden, with two novices in white veils at one end and Mother Mary Joseph at the other. One by one, they welcomed the new arrival to Carmel and wished her much joy.

A nun who appeared to be in her late thirties introduced herself as Sister Elizabeth, then presented Helen with a copy of *The Interior Castle,* Saint Teresa of Avila's spiritual masterpiece. Sister Christine, a nun about the same age, leaned in and stage-whispered, "She's giving it to you so someone will finally tell her what's in it."

Sister Elizabeth shooed her away. "Do we have to let the new girl see what we're like *so soon?*"

A middle-aged nun with the bluest eyes Helen had ever seen handed her a bouquet of wildflowers and said, "Welcome to God's hidden garden. I am Sister Emmanuel."

"She's our infirmarian," Sister Elizabeth explained, "and

I'm the refectorian. She's very good at her job, which I take credit for, because I'm so bad at mine. I give her plenty of cases to learn from."

"That's not true!" Sister Emmanuel protested. "Only that one time, really." Several of the nuns laughed out loud when they heard this, leading one of them to warn, "If we don't pipe down, the neighbors might call the police."

"Our neighbors *are* the police," Sister Elizabeth reminded her, pointing in the direction of the Academy, and the laughter got even louder.

The only nun who did not seem affected by all of the levity was a tall woman who prayed the rosary as she waited in the reception line. When it came her turn to greet the new Sister, she introduced herself as Sister Anne and said, "May you find the strength to do God's will and to leave your own preferences behind," making it sound like an admonishment rather than a blessing.

An elderly, nearly blind Sister took the new postulant's hands into her own, squeezed them gently, and smiled, then passed her to Mother Mary Joseph without a word. The peace in the old woman's face, Helen thought, was as eloquent as any speech.

With the introductions completed, the prioress announced, "Today is the Feast of the Triumph of the Cross. Earlier this morning we prayed, 'In the cross we are victorious, through the cross we shall reign, by the cross all evil is destroyed.'

"As peaceful as our life may seem here, we are not here to escape the cross. We are here to bear it out of love for Our Lord. Our whole lives are a reaching out to the One who died on the cross for us. The miracle of it is, we only feel the weight of the cross when we try to get out from under it. If we bear it gratefully, we find that *it carries us*. We wish our new Sister much joy."

At the sound of another bell, the nuns folded their hands under their sleeves and lowered their gazes. Their faces went neutral, as if they had all become invisible to one another, then they drifted away, leaving Sister Helen and her novice mistress alone in the garden. "It's manual labor period now," Sister Teresa whispered. "You'll be working in the kitchen today. Once again, follow me."

On their way they passed by the sacristy, where Sister Anne, the nun who had been so serious earlier, was already laying out the priest's vestments for ironing. She seemed unaware that she was being watched.

"Sacristan is the most demanding assignment," Sister Teresa explained when they had turned the corner into the refectory. "She must be willing to work like Martha, who toiled so that Mary could worship at the Lord's feet. It takes a special sort of person to do that job well. Sister Anne does it *extremely* well."

Sensing a fracture in the compliment, Helen confided in Sister Teresa, "I felt like she was looking right through me. As if she didn't expect me to last very long here."

Sister Teresa laughed. "Then just think of the satisfaction you'll have when you prove her wrong."

When they reached the kitchen, Sister Teresa showed her where the utensils were kept, explained how the community shared the burden of preparing food and washing the dishes, then led her to a butcher-block table piled high with vegetables. "You wash and cut those, and I'll start preparing the stock for the soup." She handed Helen a knife, and pointed to a colander hanging over the sink.

The colander reminded Helen of the night her grandfather died. At the time, his death had seemed to lead her away from God, but now it struck her with the force of revelation that the very opposite was true. Sister Priscilla had been right:

God knows what he's doing, even when we don't.

"Helen, come quick. It's about to start."

"I'll be there in a second."

"Hurry, or you'll miss it."

Her grandmother spent most of her days and nights lying in bed watching television now. She seemed to have aged ten years in the months since the funeral.

"Here it is!"

It was Christmas Eve, and the Apollo 8 astronauts were about to broadcast live pictures as they orbited the moon. Helen came upstairs and watched from the doorway. The bluish light from the set made the bedroom look like a grotto carved out of an iceberg.

"Don't you want me to open the curtains, Grandma?"

"Then I can't see the picture, it's too glary. Look!"

The screen got fuzzy for a moment, then sharpened to reveal an airless, colorless, scarred world. When the astronauts pointed their camera up, away from the lunar horizon and toward the earth, they abandoned their usual technical language in favor of poetry, taking turns reading from the first ten chapters of Genesis. The last astronaut to read signed off with the words, "And from the crew of Apollo 8, we close with good night, good luck, a Merry Christmas, and God bless all of you—all of you on the good earth."

When the broadcast ended, Helen followed the stairs to her old room and found herself staring at the uneven ceiling again. The good earth? From a distance, maybe. Up close it didn't look so great.

That night she dreamt of visiting the moon as an astronaut and finding Sister Priscilla already there, knocking chalk out of her erasers. "What are you doing here?" she asked the nun, whose habit apparently doubled as a space suit.

"Showing God what I'm capable of," Sister Priscilla answered, whacking the erasers together until she disappeared in a cloud of moon dust.

When Helen woke up, it was still dark out. Venus, the morning star, shone right outside her window like a beacon, reminding her that it was Christmas. Her dream about Sister Priscilla made her wish she could see her former teacher again. She hadn't visited the school since graduating earlier that year, and had not gone to church since then, either. Helen remembered that the Sisters at St. Ina's always met in chapel for Mass at six in the morning. Would they be there even on Christmas?

She looked at Venus again, and the urge to visit the nun got stronger. Perhaps it was nostalgia for a time, before death broke up what little family she had left, when she believed that a personal, loving God watched over us all, or maybe it was just an excuse to get out of the house. Sears was closed for the holidays, so she would not be going to work. Her only plans for the day were to do laundry and cook dinner.

She got dressed and drove the five miles to the school, but then froze at the sight of the crucifix mounted over the door to the chapel.

There it is, she thought, the symbol we're supposed to cherish above all others. The most innocent man in the world, nailed to a cross to die.

She watched from the car as parishioners, bundled up against the cold, stamped the snow out of their shoes and filed into the chapel. A bell rang six times to mark the hour. She either had to go in or go home.

It was peaceful in the car. No sermons, no military-themed hymns, no gory images. On the other hand, if she didn't believe in any of it anymore, what was there to be afraid of? She had come to see Sister Priscilla, not wrestle with Catholicism. Couldn't she just watch the service as if it were a scene in a movie?

She hurried in before she could change her mind. The chapel was nearly full, with the nuns in their starched habits spread out among

88

the more colorfully dressed parishioners. Helen found a seat in the back and tried to figure out which of the draped shoulders belonged to Sister Priscilla. Her eyes were drawn to one figure whose back looked straighter than the others'; when the congregation stood for the priest's entrance, Helen glimpsed the nun's face, and her guess was confirmed. Sister Priscilla had to have attended thousands of services by then, yet she looked as attentive as a convert waiting to be baptized.

On the wall next to Sister Priscilla hung one of the Stations of the Cross, a wooden sculpture depicting Christ's body being lowered into his mother's arms. Helen tried not to look at it.

Pretend it's just a movie, she reminded herself, but even as a movie the story was too distressing to ignore. God cast in the role of offended parent who had to be flattered and mollified, man as the ungrateful child who spoiled the world for everyone and everything by having once chosen curiosity over obedience. It was a choice that could hardly have come as a surprise to his omniscient Father, who gave the man curiosity and free will in the first place.

It's a mean story, Helen fumed. An absentee father who demands that his children put him at the center of their lives and beg for his return. Sister Priscilla didn't think it was mean, apparently. She was so in love with God that she had married him, even though she would not see his face, hear his voice, or feel his embrace for as long as she lived. One of us, Helen thought, is flying blind.

After reading from the Gospel, the priest dedicated his Christmas homily to the astronauts and asked the congregation to pray for their safe return.

"The good earth," the priest quoted. "That's how the astronauts described the view from out there. The good earth isn't a place, though. It's a state of mind. It's how the earth looks if you try to see it from God's perspective.

"Most of the time, we place ourselves at the center of the world, and expect it all to revolve around us. The view can look pretty bleak from there." His eyes met Helen's. "On the other hand, if we put God at the center of everything, the view changes completely."

Helen felt like a bird that had just flown into a pane of glass, and her thoughts tumbled in the confusion. Instead of feeling trapped in a theater showing a bad movie, she saw herself as the projector.

Could it be that I'm the one who has it wrong?

She felt a touch on her shoulder. "Is that Helen Nye I see?"

Mass was over. Sister Priscilla stood in the row behind her, her cheek painted with light from one of the stained-glass windows. She was dazzling to look at, a votive candle come to life. "Merry Christmas, Helen."

Helen distrusted her feelings. For all she knew, this sense of inversion would fade as soon as she got outside, where reality waited for her. "Something happened during Mass, Sister."

"Something good or bad?"

"I don't know. Strange."

"Maybe it's because you're here. Holy Family's your regular church, isn't it?"

"Yes. But I woke up this morning and felt like I should come here. I don't know why."

Sister Priscilla paused to examine Helen's face, then she smiled. "He's after you."

At the end of her first day at Carmel, humbled by the depth of the Great Silence, Sister Helen went into her cell, undressed, and crawled under the serge sheets. They itched against her skin.

The day had gone smoothly. In choir, she had not lost her place or made any noise during page turns, and she managed to sing in tune. She could sense the others' approval even without looking at them; one tone-deaf nun could turn communal praise into a daily scourging.

Now she stared up at the ceiling, pleased to see that it was not slanted like the ceiling of her old bedroom. All of the lines in the room were ordered, symmetrical, even. She had no regrets about leaving the world of her childhood behind, but wondered what sort of cross God had in mind for her in this one. Would it be boredom? Loneliness? Fear? She'd read *A Nun's Story;* she knew that religious life wasn't for everyone. The silence and austerity could drive a woman to despair. Sometimes even those with genuine vocations failed God's test.

When I see my cross, will I run from it?

The sound of a wooden clapper drove a wedge through the silence. Before the echo had died away, Mother Mary

Joseph delivered the retiring sentence for the evening, chosen from the next day's liturgy:

> *Will your wonders be known in the dark*
> *or your justice in the land of oblivion?*

Sister Helen lay awake in the perfect stillness for hours. The mystery of God both drew and frightened her.

1982

The Desert

Our Lady
of Mount Carmel

The sun turned the choir into a furnace.

Thirteen foreheads glistened; damp fingers stuck to the pages of breviaries. The brown Carmelite habit was designed to keep nuns alive during the harsh European winters, but in Los Angeles in July, it made each day a rehearsal for death.

> *Lord, hear my prayer;*
> *let my cry come to You.*
> *Do not hide Your face from me*
> *now that I am in distress.*

Thirteen years had passed since Sister John came to Carmel, and now her heart felt squeezed dry. God thirsted, but she had nothing to offer. The Gregorian melodies, sung without harmony, sounded like dirges. Her arms ached, her back felt sore, and she was hungry. Each Hour in choir was a desert to be crossed on her knees. Mirages of peace shimmered and beckoned, only to recede as her spirit approached. There was no shade, no shelter, no water.

> *For my days vanish like smoke;*
> > *my bones burn away as in a furnace.*
> *I am withered, dried up like grass,*
> > *too wasted to eat my food.*

Her first six years as a nun had passed quickly. A contemplative had to relearn nearly everything, from how to walk, to how to eat, to how to think. She had to master hundreds of rituals and traditions until they became second nature, orient herself to the liturgical calendar, and train herself to read, pray, and even remember with her heart as opposed to her mind. She went to bed every night exhausted and woke up every morning hungry, which taught her to place less emphasis on comfort. The rigorous daily schedule, which seemed to allow for no personal freedom, taught her to measure freedom differently. In religious life, everything was turned either upside down or inside out: to gain, one had to lose everything first. The only path to victory was through surrender. To become full, one had to become empty.

She named herself John of the Cross after the Spanish mystic and poet who, along with Saint Teresa of Avila, had dedicated himself to the spiritual reform of the Carmelite order. Denounced, imprisoned, beaten, and even excommunicated for his efforts, he never lost faith in the insights the Holy Spirit gave him. During his incarceration in Toledo, he wrote several lyric poems, including *The Dark Night,* which described the soul's crucifying but purifying journey away from self and toward God. As Sister John of the Cross, she hoped that when she faced her own dark night of the soul, she would, like her patron saint, find the strength to choose faith over despair.

After six years of training and a feeling of steady progress toward God, she made Solemn Profession—vows of chastity, poverty, and obedience that could be revoked only through special dispensation from the Vatican. Solemn Profession was the Carmelites' only public ritual; on that occasion the nuns removed the screen between the chapel and the choir and became visible to the congregation. On the day of her ceremony, Sister John saw only one familiar face in the chapel: Sister Priscilla had made the trip from Ohio to wish her well. They were allowed to visit with each other in the parlor for the rest of the day, separated by the grille, but able to speak and hold hands through the bars. Her former teacher departed with the words, "You'll be in my prayers always, Sister John," and then the reality of the transformation sank in: Helen was no longer waiting for her life to begin. The great journey was under way.

After Solemn Profession, however, rites of passage in the spiritual life suddenly thinned out. For seven years she watched as the cloister got smaller and the silence got bigger. She was a bride of Christ, but still had not met her Spouse, and the farther she traveled inward without finding Him, the more aware she became of His absence.

> *I am like a desert owl,*
>> *like an owl among the ruins.*
> *I lie awake and moan,*
>> *like a lone sparrow on the roof.*

The Hour concluded with a sigh. The Sisters filed out of choir in order of seniority, with the oldest Sister at the front of the line and the youngest taking up the rear. Sister John kept pace with the veil in front of her, thinking, *I've been walking behind Sister Angelica for thirteen years. Only our deaths will change the order. Or if one of us leaves.*

More and more often she found herself thinking of the novices and postulants who had decided that they did not, after all, have genuine vocations. She also thought of the two professed Sisters she had known who had asked to be released from vows. One of them, after twenty-five years of service to God, had fallen in love with a priest. After exhaustive correspondence with the Holy See and the Vatican and a year of painful waiting, dispensation was withheld in her case and she was told to pray. In the end, she left the community disappointed and bitter, her soul in a state of mortal sin.

Sister John also found herself thinking of Sister Agatha,

who had gone to God, but who surely had deserved a better death. Intractable pain had robbed this gentlest of nuns of the opportunity to review her life at its end and surrender with a peaceful heart.

These were dangerous thoughts, Sister John knew, but she also knew that if she had any doubts about her vocation, this was the time to deal with them. A woman could leave the convent in her early thirties and still have time for marriage and children, but every day she postponed the decision, the window of opportunity got smaller.

It was during this period of spiritual aridity that she learned why cloistered nuns laughed so much. In a place where one was never allowed to forget the urgency, difficulty, and seriousness of one's mission, sneezes became pratfalls. Truly funny moments could be savored for weeks, and some were cherished to the point that Sisters only had to look at each other a certain way to invoke their memory. One afternoon the mailman delivered a letter addressed, in a child's innocent handwriting, to "St. Joseph's Disgraced Carmelites." Mother Mary Joseph nearly had to declare a cell day—a day off—because it seemed that no one was going to be able to stop laughing in time for choir. On another day, Sister Angelica, who had spilled some dishwashing liquid on the toaster and shorted it out, stood up during Faults and announced gravely, "I wish to proclaim myself for wasting Joy and blowing a fuse."

Sister John entertained herself with these memories as she

waited in her cell for the call to Vespers, then got up to use the bathroom. Another Sister with the same idea approached from the opposite direction. A moment of awkwardness ensued. Wanting to practice humility, Sister John pulled back to allow the other nun to use the bathroom first, but this younger Sister's humility would not allow it, and the struggle began.

The two nuns stood with eyes downcast, signing politely with their hands:

Excuse me.

You first.

No, you. Please.

Just standing there forever! Was that not a fault against poverty, since both nuns were wasting time that could have been used for prayer? Sister John felt as if she had wandered onstage during a performance of the Passion Play, only to realize that she had forgotten all of her lines. She yielded and stepped into the bathroom first, but when she came back out, the novice was gone. Mother Mary Joseph was standing in her place.

Please, you come, she signed. She led the way to the kitchen, closed the door behind them, and asked Sister John to sit down.

"What is it, Mother?"

"We have a visitor at the Turn asking to speak to you."

The Turn was a small, revolving window that allowed the nuns to receive mail and exchange gifts without being seen.

Sister John thought she had never seen Mother Mary Joseph look so serious. "Is it bad news?" she asked, her heart pounding.

The prioress shook her head. "It's your mother."

Sister John looked at the pots and ladles hanging over the stove, at the mixing bowls filled with dough and covered with damp cloths, and at the magnets on the refrigerator holding recipe cards, and thought: I never saw my mother in a kitchen. "What should I do?" she asked, feeling numb.

"Did you have any idea that she would be coming?"

"No."

The executor of Sister John's grandparents' estate, a family friend, had written some time ago with the news that he'd tracked down an address for Sister John's mother. She lived in San Diego, only two hours' drive from the Carmel of St. Joseph, and had an unfamiliar last name: Barnard. At first Sister John had resisted the urge to contact her, partly out of resentment, but also thinking it might reopen the wounds of her childhood and make life at the cloister even harder. Eventually, however, curiosity won out. She wrote a letter explaining who she was and where she lived, emphasizing that she was cloistered and dedicated to prayer and forgiveness, then watched the Turn at mail time every day for weeks, hoping for a response. None had come.

"What did she look like?"

Mother Emmanuel tried to smile. "I only heard her voice."

"Did she sound drunk?"

"Not that I could tell." Mother Emmanuel leaned forward, distancing herself from the cross on the wall just behind her. "Would you like me to ask her to come another time? When you've had some chance to prepare?"

Sister John's mouth felt dry. "I wouldn't know how to prepare for this. I might as well go see her now."

She walked into the parlor and sat down in the lone chair on the nuns' side of the room. A closed curtain hid the metal grille separating the enclosure side from the visitor's side. She heard the prioress speaking through the Turn, instructing her mother to open the door to her right. The curtain in front of her trembled as someone entered the parlor. They were only a few feet apart now.

What am I going to say to her? How should I be?

She wanted to go through this experience as a nun, secure in faith and in God's peace, not as a shaky, conflicted daughter, but her feelings were not under her control. She took hold of the curtain and slid it to one side. The visitor's area of the parlor was furnished with a chair, an end table with a vase of wildflowers on it, and a crucifix. A window looked out toward the driveway, and on its sill dozed a cat that the community's extern nun had rescued from the pound. The end of its tail twitched.

Her mother sat in the chair, her hands folded stiffly on her lap, a purse on the floor next to her. She wore a cream-colored skirt and blazer, and her shoes matched her suit perfectly. Sister John remembered her mother from old photographs as having brown hair, like her own, but now it was gray and styled in a soft pageboy cut. Professional but friendly. Her mother wore plain gold earrings and a simple necklace, all tasteful, but then spoiled the effect with an enamel brooch pin shaped like a seal, balancing a rhinestone heart on its nose.

Sister John recognized her mother's face, but nothing else fit. Which, she realized, was probably exactly what her mother was thinking, seeing her grown daughter for the first time in the Carmelite habit.

"Praised be Jesus Christ," she said.

Her mother reached into her purse, pulled out a tissue, and held it on her lap. "Hello, Helen." Her inflection sounded rehearsed.

Sister John couldn't think of anything nunlike to say, so she said, "You look a lot better off than I expected." Her mother smiled, but Sister John didn't smile back. As the initial surprise wore off, she began feeling angry. "This is certainly a surprise."

Her mother crushed the tissue into a ball. "Maybe I shouldn't have come."

"Why did you? Why didn't you write first?"

The cat dropped down from the sill and rubbed itself against the visitor's legs. She reached down to pet it, appearing relieved to have something to do with her hands. "For a long time I thought it would be better if you didn't hear from me at all."

"Better?" Sister John asked, her face feeling hot. "Better than what?"

"I was very immature when you were born, Helen. I wasn't ready to be a parent—I wasn't even ready to be an adult. I panicked. That's the only way I can describe it."

"Twenty-seven years is a long time to be panicked."

Her mother dabbed at her eyes with the ball of tissue. "It's more complicated than that. I met someone when you were very small, and I put off telling him about you because I was afraid. I knew he wasn't ready for kids, and I didn't want to lose him. I didn't plan on this getting so far out of hand; I thought the right time would come and that we would all be a family together, but I was more of a coward than I thought. Then I got pregnant and our daughter was born, and I was even more afraid. What if he left me then? I had already been a failure as a mother once, I couldn't do that again. I knew it was wrong, but I felt it was the only way."

The wall clock hummed. "I have a sister?"

"And a brother." She took out a fresh tissue. "They're wonderful people, not like me. Please don't hold what I've done against them."

"Do they know about me?"

Her mother's expression hardened. "I'm not excusing what I did. I'm a mother who abandoned her child so she could have a shiny new life. That's always the person I'll be, no matter what else I do, and I'm not proud of it. I came here to tell you the truth so that you could finally put me out of your mind. I thought it might give you some closure. It's not much, but it's something."

Now Sister John realized why her mother had come: this was an opportunity to end the relationship once and for all, and to get away with the lie. She was asking her abandoned daughter not only to forgive the deception, but to cooperate with it so that the healthy family wouldn't be disturbed. Her mother didn't want any more letters coming to the house, that was the bottom line.

Sister John wondered what the most devastating thing a daughter could say to her mother could possibly be. Something came to mind, a harpoon with a barb at the end so it could never be pulled out, but just as she prepared to drive it into her mother's heart, she noticed the seal brooch again.

It was such a tasteless piece of jewelry that it made her hesitate. Her mother was a manipulative, selfish monster; everything about her was calculated, from the tone of her voice to the posing with tissues to make herself appear vulnerable, but the pin was a failure no matter how you looked at it.

Failure—the word stopped her cold.

Had she forgotten so soon that she was supposed to love as Christ loved? Her mother wasn't here to mend fences, she was asking a favor. Sister John thought: If I deny this request, it would only be to hurt my mother, to get revenge, and it would bring pain to her other children. What positive purpose would it serve? I'm a cloistered nun, my half-siblings wouldn't be able to have much of a relationship with me anyway. Maybe right here—not in choir or in my cell—is where I find out what my vows were all about.

"What are their names?" she asked her mother.

After a pause, "Beth and Ethan."

"Do you have pictures of them?"

After another pause, her mother searched her purse, took out an unevenly trimmed photograph, and brought it to the grille. She held it sideways and passed it between the bars. Sister John took it back to her chair.

The two siblings stood by the side of a road under a billboard for some kind of tourist attraction. It looked like a hot, overcast day somewhere on the East Coast—the billboard cast no shadow. It read, "Keep yelling, kids! They'll stop!" Beth, who looked about fifteen, had blond hair and a small frame. She posed with the sign like a game-show hostess, while her younger brother kept his hands tucked in the pockets of his shorts, affecting nonchalance. He had a round face and the same dimpled knees Sister John had had at his age. His brown hair was tousled, as if he had been sleeping in the car just before the picture was taken.

Sister John stared at the picture for a long time. When she passed it back through the grille, she saw that her mother's hands were shaking. "Knowing their names means I can pray for their health and happiness every day."

Her mother struggled with the wallet and purse as she put the photograph away. She looked pathetic, not monstrous.

"I'm glad to know the truth. Be at peace now, Mother, and go with God."

Sister John kept her eyes lowered as she slid the curtain shut. She measured her steps as she left the parlor, and made sure to open and close the door gently. Mother Mary Joseph stood just outside, waiting, but Sister John could not face her just then. She hurried out to the garden, past the roses and the fountain and the ginkgo tree, until she knew she was out of sight. She pulled off her wimple and veil, squatted down against the wall, and buried her face in her hands.

Thirteen years of searching for the deeper meaning of faith and suffering evaporated in an instant. Even then, God remained silent.

1994

Rain from Heaven

Holy Thursday

The choir stalls kept the most perfect vigil of all: waiting to serve. Emptiness was their gift.

> *Spring rains, bare altar;*
> *Christ was obedient, accepting even death.*

Sister John dropped to her knees at the far end of the choir and began scrubbing toward the altar. Good Friday was only hours away; the community would be making the journey to Calvary along with Christ in that very room, so the job had to be done right.

> *Floor, water, sponge.*
> *One breath, one stroke:*
>   *one more shiny scallop.*

Sister John's vocation had survived the test of her mother's visit, not because she was able to interpret the event in the light of faith, but because it changed the way she felt about drudgery. Thought generated suffering; industry drowned it out. She threw herself on God's mercy and lost herself in work, and as her sense of personal ambition withered, so did her doubts.

The line of time turned into a circle; years repeated themselves along with the cycle of liturgy. On the twentieth anniversary of her arrival at the cloister, when she was forty years old, she stood up at recreation and announced that it felt as if she'd been at Carmel for just a few hours. "I entered on the morning of the Triumph of the Cross," she said, "and here it is, evening of the same day. Saint Teresa was right—all things pass, but God never changes."

> *Tired shoulders, half-empty pail.*
> *Sister Angelica wants to scatter rocks*
> *around the altar.*
> *Not on my floor!*

She straightened up to find Sister Anne standing in the doorway, watching. The older nun pointed to the clock on the wall, indicating that half an hour remained until Vespers, then signed, *Please, you help me.* Sister John nodded, put away her cleaning materials, then joined Sister Anne in the sacristy.

The sacristan lifted an alb and a stole from the vesture

drawer in the sacristy and laid them out on a table. She examined them for stains or loose threads, then signed for Sister John to iron them while she prepared the floral arrangements. Making a silent prayer for vocations to the priesthood, Sister John watched the fabric smooth out behind the iron like flour. Next, she put the freshened garments on hangers and carried them over to the double-door storage shelves linking the enclosed part of the monastery to the chapel. After ringing a small bell, she opened the doors and passed the vestments through to Sister Mary Michael.

The extern had some questions for Sister Anne about decorating the sanctuary. Sister John took advantage of this opportunity to sit down and close her eyes. The effort of scrubbing, or perhaps the smell of the floor cleaner, had triggered one of her headaches. Her doctor suspected that these headaches were either migraines or the result of overzealous fasting, and suggested that for Lent she try giving up the idea of giving things up. She took his advice and ate as heartily as the monastic diet would allow, but the headaches still troubled her, so the diagnosis of migraine won out.

When Sister John opened her eyes again, Sister Anne was already stripping the altar of its old linen. Sister John got up and helped center a fresh cloth over the *mensa*, letting all four sides hang to within an inch of the floor. This style of altar covering, known as a Jacobean cloth, required no extra decoration, but Sister Anne had prepared a special touch for Easter: she had sewn a white satin fall just for this occasion, which she asked Sister John to hold in place while she stepped back to examine it.

Sister Anne squinted and leaned, as if hoping to straighten out the hem with body English, then signaled that the right side needed to be higher. Sister John raised it a quarter of an inch, then began pinning in the corrections, but the headache intensified and made it difficult to concentrate.

> *How many to go? Don't look.*
> *One breath, pierce.*
> *Second breath, out the other side.*
> *Third breath, new pin.*

The left side of her vision got blurry, and her fingers felt stiff. The doctor had assured her that these were common migraine symptoms, and that the best thing to do when the headaches struck was not to struggle against them. "Just try to relax," he said, "breathe deeply and let it happen. Surrender to it. You're a contemplative; think of it as a spiritual exercise."

> *Remember what Christ endured.*
> *Hang on.*

One of the pins slipped out of her hand, ringing like a miniature triangle as it bounced on the floor. All of a sudden, her pain disappeared. This was new; the headaches usually took hours to run their course. She looked down toward the floor and saw that it looked impossibly distant, like an image in a funhouse mirror. Instead of frightening her, the sight filled her with an irresistible, dreamy curiosity. When she reached down toward the pin, her hand looked strangest of all, as if it belonged to someone else. She willed herself to move it, one finger at a time.

But where is the willing coming from?

Her mind felt like a mirror; everything in it came from somewhere else. The silence in the room came alive, like the positive space in a Chinese landscape painting, or the words left out of a poem. Something buried so deep inside her that she had forgotten it was there rose to the surface.

How long, O Lord, will you forget me?
How long will you hide your face?

Loneliness, the hole in the center of her being.

Look at me, answer me, Lord my God!

The response came in the form of understanding, and it came all at once, as if a dam had burst in her soul. Her search for God had been like a hand trying to grasp itself. God, who is infinite, cannot *become* present because He can never *be* absent.

You were here all along

"Sister? Are you not feeling well?" God was present in Sister Anne's voice, He was present in her face.

Nothing was changed, yet everything was changed. Compared to this, she felt as if she had been sleepwalking all her life. "God is here," she answered. She picked up the pin and guided it through the fabric.

> *I pierce the universe.*
> *God pierces me.*
> *I do not think; I am thought.*
> *I do not know; I am known.*

Every movement, every breath was poetry. She had passed through her dark night of the soul, and understood now how the light in one's heart—the light of faith—could shine brighter than the midday sun. When the bell rang for private prayer, she went to the scriptorium to get a notebook. She brought it back to her cell, closed the door, and watched in amazement and joy as light poured out of her onto the pages.

1997

Darkness

Peter Claver, Priest

Two squirrels raced down the trunk of the sycamore tree and halted on a branch. They twitched their tails without looking directly at each other, then spiraled back up into the canopy.

I made a commitment to live by faith, not by reason.

The ever-changing pattern of jet trails overhead was the only visible reminder that the cloister occupied a specific place and time in the world.

Leaves against sky. Green for Ordinary time, blue for the Marian feasts. The Blessed Virgin's mantle of compassion embracing the world. Sister John had promised to announce the results of her medical tests to the community following the Mass of Our Lady of Sorrows. She had several days until then to meditate and pray on the news in private, and to decide what to do.

I felt so empty for so long, Lord, but I did not turn my back on you. I gave up everything to search for you, and when I had lost everything, you found me. How could I ever doubt you?

From the materials the doctor had given her, she learned that temporal-lobe epilepsy sometimes caused changes in behavior and thinking even when the patient was not having seizures. These changes included hypergraphia (voluminous writing), an intensification but also a narrowing of emotional response, and an obsessive interest in religion and philosophy. The novelist Dostoevsky, who was epileptic, followed this model so closely that the syndrome was eventually named after him.

"There are moments," Dostoevsky wrote, "and it is only a matter of five or six seconds, when you feel the presence of the eternal harmony . . . a terrible thing is the frightful clearness with which it manifests itself and the rapture with which it fills you. If this state were to last more than five seconds, the soul could not endure it and would have to disappear. During these five seconds I live a whole human existence, and for that I would give my whole life and not think that I was paying too dearly . . ."

The similarity to her own experiences was unmistakable. If Dostoevsky had been given the option of treatment, she wondered, would he have taken it? *Should* he have?

The article went on to speculate that other gifted artists and writers may have suffered from the disorder. Van Gogh, Tennyson, and Proust were mentioned as likely candidates, along with Socrates, Saint Paul, and Saint Teresa of Avila.

Saint Teresa's seizures—along with her heart attacks, chronic nausea, and even a three-day coma—were a matter of Church record. No one agonized more than she over the question of how to tell the difference between genuine spiritual experiences and false ones. At one point she even feared for her own sanity, but after being assured by Saint Peter of Alcantara that her spiritual favors were from God, she never again lost confidence in her visions, even after being denounced to the Inquisition.

Teresa called illness her greatest teacher, but she also warned against seeking illness as a means of cultivating holiness. She saw doctors for her maladies; when she wrote about turning suffering into opportunities for grace, she was almost certainly talking about incurable illness. She exhorted her readers to stay as healthy as possible so that they could all serve God to the best of their abilities.

But if looking after the body was so important, Sister John wondered, why hadn't Christ answered Pilate's questions and spared himself execution? Wasn't the point of his sacrifice to inspire the rest of us to place faith before self-concern?

If what you have shown me these past three years has all been a mirage, then I am worse off now than I ever was. If I lose my sense of you, I lose everything.

Thirteenth Friday in Ordinary Time

Father Aaron was the parish priest assigned to administer sacraments to the nuns. He celebrated Mass every morning in the small chapel, delivering the Eucharist to each Sister through a window in the screen, but otherwise had little contact with them. He was a large man with eyebrows that patrolled his forehead like gray battleships, ready to meet any threat to his parishioners' souls. Heart trouble sapped much of his strength, but whenever he led Mass, it seemed as if the Holy Spirit itself rushed into him and gave him vitality.

Father Aaron toed the line when it came to Vatican policy, and some of the Sisters complained of a patronizing attitude toward female religious. He believed in grace and the power of contemplative prayer, but was also fond of quoting Solomon's warning against too strong a desire for miracles:

"What need has a man to desire and seek what is above his natural capacity?" He was not someone whom Sister John would normally consult for spiritual advice, but these were not normal circumstances. She'd heard her doctor's opinion; now she wanted to hear from a professional religious, someone far enough from the situation to be objective. Also, she knew that a nun's preferences with regard to spiritual direction could sometimes reflect where she *wanted* to be led rather than where God was trying to lead her. Deciding to keep an open mind, and thinking that Solomon's warning might, after all, be relevant to her situation, she sent Father Aaron a note asking for a meeting.

The moment he took his place across the grille from her in the parlor, his nose began whistling as he breathed through it.

"God bless you, Sister. Your prayers sustain us. How can I be of assistance?"

"God bless you, Father. I seek the grace of your counsel."

A long, thoughtful whistle. "What troubles you?"

She confided her diagnosis and her struggle to sort out God's will from her own in the matter of how to deal with the illness. "I want to make the right decision," she said, "but I feel confused. Should I automatically assume that my mystical experiences have been false, or should I stand behind what my heart tells me? Is God asking me to let go of concerns for my health, or is he asking me to let go of my desire for his presence?"

Father Aaron's chin rested against his chest, and the

whistling had ceased. She couldn't see whether his eyes were open or closed.

"Father?"

He raised his head slowly and began to swell in his chair, like a balloon receiving an infusion of helium. "Take heart, Sister!" he boomed. "You may feel separated from grace right now, but in reality you are probably closer to it now than you ever were before."

She hadn't expected to hear this. "How could that be?"

"Because we're all better off having doubts about the state of our souls than presuming ourselves to be holy." His eyebrows moved ominously, as if they had sighted the enemy at last. "You allowed yourself to think that loving God meant enjoying His company, having ecstasies. It was all about *you,* wasn't it? But loving God is supposed to be all about *Him.* About trusting Him, putting yourself in His hands completely." He sank back into the chair, folding his arms over his stomach. He had almost as much hair on the backs of his fingers as above his eyes. "The problem is, you're still looking out for number one. What comes before the number one, Sister?"

This, she realized, was the patronizing manner the other Sisters complained about. "Zero."

He nodded. "That's right. Which is the same as infinity. If we subtract ourselves from the equation, we find that God is left." His eyebrows drifted apart, the dangerous part of their mission accomplished.

She wanted a direct answer, not more metaphors. She had too many of those already. "You're recommending the surgery, then?"

Whistle, whistle. "The decision has to come from you, otherwise it won't mean anything. I'm recommending an attitude, which I'll sum up like this: God first, others second, me last. As long as you stick to that, you can be assured you'll make the right decision."

John Chrysostom, Bishop and Doctor

What if I have it all upside down? What if I am the one who knows nothing of God, and the people in the world are actually interceding on my behalf with their ordinary, daily struggles?

In spite of his condescending manner, Father Aaron had raised a question that Sister John could not ignore. What if her whole approach to spirituality was, indeed, selfish? What if it was true that her idea of loving God meant "enjoying His company"? That would explain her resistance to the idea of giving up her seizures, and it might even explain the surprising popularity of her book. Most people want to be told they can have what they want, and wasn't that what Sister John was telling them? That direct experiences of God are available to everyone?

If every path led to you, there would be no need for redemption, no need to choose love over self-love, no possibility of being mistaken. Have I been worshiping projections of my own neediness?

Of the two hermitages at the far end of the enclosure, Sister John preferred the one at the southwest corner. Bamboo surrounded it so that, looking out the window, one felt transported to a mountain retreat in Asia. No one was scheduled to use it that month, so Sister John, hoping a change of surroundings might freshen her perspective, decided to spend the hour of private prayer there.

The hermitage was smaller than her cell, and even more sparsely furnished. She pushed the door open, felt along the wall for the light switch, then cried out involuntarily. Someone was already lying on the cot, with her back to the door.

A white veil covered her head.

"I'm so sorry, I didn't—" A second shock passed through her. "Sister? Are you all right?"

Nothing moved under the brown and white fabric.

"Sister!"

"Praised be Jesus Christ," Sister Miriam mumbled into the pillow.

Sister John's relief was short-lived. When a novice so close to taking vows looked this upset, something was wrong.

"May He be forever praised . . . what's wrong?"

"I'll be fine."

"Would you like to talk with someone?"

No response. Remembering their conversation in the scriptorium, Sister John asked, "Is it about your parents?"

Sister Miriam started to shake her head, then burst into tears. Sister John sat down in the chair at the foot of the bed and waited. Outside the window, a pair of cedar waxwings feasted on pyracantha berries.

Sister Miriam cried herself out, then took a tissue out of her pocket and blew her nose.

"I can see that you're struggling," Sister John said. "I've had my share of bad days here, too."

Sister Miriam sat up slowly, hugging her arms across her chest. "They were just here," she said, speaking so quietly that Sister John could barely hear her. "They think this is a cult."

"Do they think we're keeping you here against your will?"

She nodded. "I tried to explain that I could leave anytime, but my father pointed at the grille and asked what the bars were for."

"Did you explain to him?"

She nodded again. "I told him they were just symbolic, and he said, 'They're symbolic, all right. Where else do you see bars on windows, and people living in cells?'"

"Does your mother feel the same way?"

"I don't know. In our family, my father tells everybody else how to think."

Sister John thought of how conscientious Sister Miriam was, yet how tentative, and it began to make sense. Sister

Miriam threw the tissue into the wastebasket. "The problem is, there's always some truth to what my father says."

"You feel pressured to stay here?"

"No, that's not it." She stared out the window. "He thinks that I'm being selfish. That I want to become holy so that people will have to pay attention to me."

"That's ridiculous—you never draw attention to yourself. You're the most self-effacing person here."

Sister Miriam shook her head. "It explains why I'm so jealous."

"Who are you jealous of?"

The novice looked stricken. "Isn't it obvious? I'm jealous of *you*. How could I not be? How could anybody here not be? We're searching, but you're *finding*."

Embarrassed silence. "God loves each of us as if there were no one else on earth," Sister John said. "Believing that is the most perfect act of faith of all." Even as she said it, however, she realized it sounded like a platitude.

"Easy for you to say," the novice snapped, then she looked stricken again. "I didn't mean that. I'm upset, that's all. Please forgive me."

Sister John wanted to comfort her, but feared that anything she said would only make matters worse. "Have you spoken with Mother Emmanuel about this?"

Sister Miriam looked too exhausted to go on with the conversation. "I suppose I'll have to. I think, right now, I'd just like to be alone for a while."

"Isn't there anything I can do? I feel terrible that I wasn't aware of this earlier."

"It's my problem, not yours. I shouldn't have troubled you with it—I'm very sorry." She was sounding more like her usual self, which Sister John didn't think was a good sign. Sister Miriam adjusted her veil and stood up. "I promised Sister Bernadette I would help her spread the tarps over the eaves today. She thinks it might rain soon."

"If you knew me better, you wouldn't feel jealous," Sister John said.

Sister Miriam genuflected before the cross, then held her head evenly as she walked out of the hermitage.

Triumph of the Cross

First rain of the season.

Sister John's habit felt damp to the touch as she put it on. She listened to the drops falling on the banana palm outside her window. It was a tropical sound, reminding her that the desert is what you bring to it, a landscape of the heart. She jotted her first entry for the day in her journal:

Our twenty-eighth anniversary. I will not turn my back on You.

Water gushed out of downspouts and fanned out over paving stones. Raindrops hung from bare branches like tears on eyelashes, only to be obliterated by collisions from above. The eucalyptus trees looked as if they were being throttled by giant hands.

Angry beauty.

The liturgy of morning prayer blurred into a collage of hope and fear. Tomorrow was Our Lady of Sorrows; Sister John had one more day to reflect on her condition before sharing it with the community. She prayed for clarity through Lauds, and afterwards she skipped breakfast to remain in her stall until Terce.

Alone in the choir, she noticed the votive candles on the left side of the altar flickering. When she looked at them directly, they stopped. As soon as she averted her eyes, the flames started dancing again. A stab of pain behind her eyes confirmed what was to come.

Into Thy hands.

When the others returned for Terce, she sensed their eyes on her as she lifted her breviary to mark pages. Could they detect the heaviness in her movements?

In You, dear God, I take refuge. If it be Your will, let others' scorn be my cross.

Terce ended with five minutes of silence. On the other side of the screen, Sister Mary Michael rang the *tintinnabulum*. Heavy footsteps echoed in the building as Father Aaron strode down the aisle of the chapel and took his place at the altar.

When he began chanting the Mass, the walls, floor, and ceiling turned into a resonating body, an instrument for sacred music. His voice was a rich sienna, the color of reassurance. Sister John heard each of her Sisters' voices as if they were chanting alone: Sister Christine sounded as if her throat were lined with mother-of-pearl, while Sister Anne's voice had more texture, like a bowed instrument. Sister Angelica sang like a coloratura soprano, with modest power but intense feeling.

Sister Elizabeth sounded exuberant, while Sister Bernadette sounded resigned. Sister Miriam sounded afraid. Mother Mary Joseph's voice was mostly breath, forming a kind of white sound that helped blend the others. Mother Emmanuel seemed to anticipate the others by a fraction of a beat, like the conductor of an orchestra.

Going even deeper into the sound with her mind, she heard each voice as a rope of faith, composed of many thin strands woven together. In these strands she heard courage, fear, selfishness, and selflessness. Nearest the core of the rope, she heard the cries of children and animals in darkness, huddled together for safety.

The very center of each rope was hollow. Was this the silence of the void, or God's silence?

At the moment of the Breaking of the Host, the congregation said in unison:

Lamb of God, You take away the sins of the world.

Hearing the voices together, she perceived them as all woven together to form a tapestry, stretching not only across the world but backward and forward into time.

The tapestry lit up.

Like a piece of quartz viewed under a black light, her soul went from achromatic to beyond chromatic. Fractures and other imperfections—including her epilepsy—became irrelevant; a much deeper beauty revealed itself now.

Faith is light, doubt is shadow. If You remove the obstacles to faith, all shadows disappear.

She opened her eyes. When had she last closed them? She was lying down. She had on her white mantle, the special garment they wore for Mass, but she was not in choir.

"Are you awake, Sister?"

"Where am I?"

"You're in the infirmary. You became ill; we had to bring you here to rest." Mother Emmanuel looked tired. Tired love.

Sister Teresa stirred in the next bed. She looked bleached, like a piece of driftwood.

"Father Aaron explained your condition to me, Sister. He had to, under the circumstances. I explained it to the others."

"We are as God made us, Mother."

Mother Emmanuel sighed. "After your seizure, you were telling us how beautiful the view was, how beautiful everything was. Do you remember saying that?"

"Yes!"
The only word I will ever need again. Every breath a
Yes, every thought a Yes.

"Have you thought about what the view looked like to the rest of us, Sister?"

My trust in God alone.

"Perhaps you aren't aware of yourself during those moments," the prioress continued. "Just when God offered Himself to us through the Eucharist, you stood up and began wandering around the choir, staring at the ceiling and humming to yourself. If Sister Christine hadn't gotten to you in time, you might have walked into the screen and knocked it over. Do you remember any of that?"

Sometimes, when we follow God, we appear to cause others to
suffer. God plans everything down to the smallest detail.

The prioress rose from the chair next to the bed. "I'd like you to stay here for the rest of the day. We'll talk about this more tomorrow. In the meantime, try to get as much rest as you can."

Sister John looked to the crucifix over the door for encouragement, but instead saw a rebuke. Now that the brilliance of her seizure had faded, doubt lost its shadow-appearance and became solid again. The horizon between reality and illusion—between the spiritual and the material, between faith and self-interest, between love and self-love—vanished.

Too restless to stay in bed but forbidden to leave the infirmary, she pulled a chair up to the window and stared out at the garden. I must stay calm, she thought. As long as I'm more careful from now on, and go to my cell as soon as I feel a headache coming, I won't disturb the others again. It will mean more absences from choir, but quality of time given to God is what counts, not quantity. What if the seizures become more frequent, or more severe? What if I'm not able to work in the kitchen, or answer the Turn, or do my share of cleaning? How much inconvenience am I willing to impose on the others before wondering if this is really God's will after all?

Pineapple sage grew at the base of the fountain. The narrow crimson blossoms reminded her of the wounds on Christ's body.

Doubt is inevitable, she told herself. Saint Teresa of Avila was tormented by doubts right up until the end of her life, but she did not give in. She knew that it was better to have a dream, and pay a price for it, than to be lukewarm. Sometimes the price of following a dream includes confusion. In her diaries, Teresa often wrote, "I didn't know what to do."

Sister John thought: I can't bear the thought of going back to who I was before. I prayed and scrubbed and went through the motions with no feeling of love, only a will to keep busy. If the surgery were to take my dream away, everything I've gone through up to now would seem meaningless. I wouldn't even be able to draw inspiration from the memory of it; I couldn't face that desert again, not this late in my life.

But what is my dream? Is it really to know God, or is it to know personal happiness? Didn't Teresa also warn that the price of following a dream includes painful setbacks, even having to start all over again? Sometimes it means facing things that we think we can't face, to learn the depth of God's mystery and of our need for faith.

My God, I feel as if I am being torn apart.

That evening the air was especially dry and still. When Sister John opened the infirmary window, she could hear her Sisters chanting the Night Office as clearly as if they were chanting in the courtyard.

> *You have taken away my friends*
> *and made me hateful in their sight.*

Imprisoned, I cannot escape;
my eyes are sunken with grief.

She formed a mental picture of the choir, with all the lights turned off except for the vigil lamp at the altar and the candle illuminating the Virgin Mary's shrine. The liturgy built to a cadenza as the two sides of the choir alternated vows of submission to God's will, then halted as the Sisters took up their instruments of penance.

Alma Redemptoris Mater, qua pervia caeli

Every Saturday evening the Sisters bared their left shoulders for the chanting of the *Miserere,* an ancient psalm of repentance. The knotted leather cords of the discipline whistled through the air, then struck flesh. With each blow, the Sisters prayed for the exaltation of the Church, for peace on earth, for the souls in Purgatory, for those in the state of sin, and for all men and women in captivity. It was not enough to be sorry for past offenses, or simply to forget them. The Sisters came to Carmel to make reparation—not only for their own sins, but for every sin ever committed. Penance stripped them of self-will and self-love, not as an end in itself, but as a means of clearing away all obstructions to the love of God.

peccatorium miserere.

When the poem ended, the monastery entered the Great Silence. The nuns would be covering their shoulders and rising from their stalls.

Sister John listened as eight pairs of sandals brushed across the floor on their way to the dormitory. She waited until she heard the Caller deliver the retiring sentence in the dormitory:

But those things I used to consider gain I have now reappraised as loss in the light of Christ.

After the final clap of wood, she slipped out of the infirmary. Alone in the choir, she noticed that everything looked flat and insubstantial; the cross above the altar looked like a fresco on the wall, the vigil lamp like a photograph of a candle.

She knelt before the Eucharist, but did not pray in words. She maintained a spirit of humility and expectancy, but did not ask for anything; she felt she no longer had any right to ask God for favors. When her legs hurt too much to kneel anymore, she sat in her stall. She did not allow herself to consider going back to the infirmary, because to retreat into the oblivion of sleep would have been to let her spirit die. She was prepared for the struggle of her life. She would not leave the room until she had decided either for or against surgery, and was prepared to live with the consequences.

Jesus faced his most difficult trial—his moment of doubt—alone. He had asked his disciples to watch and pray in the garden with him, but they had all succumbed to the weakness of the flesh and fallen asleep. When the soldiers came, the disciples were surprised and fled in confusion. Because they had not watched with Jesus, they were not ready to suffer, die, and rise with him. Sister John bared her shoulder and struck herself with the discipline several times in an attempt to shake off exhaustion, but she was fighting a losing battle. At the point where she felt she was about to fall asleep, she whispered, "I'm sorry."

Her thoughts began to unravel.

Then a hand touched her shoulder, pulling her together again. Someone had entered the choir so quietly she hadn't heard.

Mother Mary Joseph signed, *I watch for you. Rest.*

The Living Rule sat down in her stall, back bent but spirit alert. It was clear she was capable of sitting through the night, and that she intended to.

Sister John resumed her vigil, feeling her strength return. The two nuns did not look at each other, but an understanding passed between them and held. They became like two life rafts lashed together on the sea. After an hour, Mother Mary Joseph stood suddenly. She did not look tired, but after paying her respects at the altar, she left the choir.

A moth, attracted by the vigil lamp, spiraled toward it as if it were trapped in an invisible nautilus. Just when it seemed sure to destroy itself on the flame, it looped out to begin a new orbit.

Footsteps approached the choir. The Living Rule returned to her stall holding a candle, followed by Mother Emmanuel. Within a few minutes the entire community, all holding candles, rallied to keep watch with Sister John. Their presence turned night into day, midnight sun at the end of the earth. Nothing was said, but the message was clear: a Sister might feel lost, but she was never alone.

When she first became a contemplative, Sister John had envisioned a relationship to "souls in need." The foundation of religious life, after all, is a commitment to look beyond oneself. She prayed for the souls of the world every day, and assumed her efforts made a difference. When it came to her Sisters, however—who were also souls in need, but whose troubles could not be visualized away so easily—she had been stingier, more guarded. She had never really done anything for them that didn't serve her own interests.

Yet here they were, staying up all night with her so she wouldn't have to struggle alone.

She had failed to discern God's will in the matter of whether or not to treat her disorder, but she had seen today how her seizures could become a burden to her Sisters. To give up her ecstasies for their sake would be, if not a spiritual decision, at least an honorable one. She looked around the room and tried to etch the scene in memory, praying that whatever her own future might be, God would reward her Sisters for their generosity of spirit. She rose, bowed to them as a signal that her vigil was over, and returned to the infirmary.

Thank you, God, and forgive me.

1997

Surrender

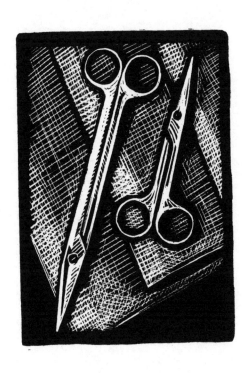

Cosmas and Damian, Martyrs

She drew the curtains around her bed, paused to stand in silence before God, then removed her habit. After putting on the hospital gown, which felt as if it were made of tissue paper, she pulled the curtain aside.

First night away from my cell in almost thirty years.
Bright room. So many sounds.

She sat at the foot of the bed and ran her fingers over the spot behind her right ear.

A medical student visited her to complete the admission paperwork. His white lab coat and badge made Sister John wish she had not changed into the hospital nightgown. Without her own version of a uniform, and with her arms and shaved head fully exposed, she felt like a plucked bird. The medical student, who was Chinese and spoke with a heavy accent, had the smoothest skin Sister John had ever seen on a man. He explained that before Sister John could sign the consent form for surgery, she had to be warned of the risks.

"With surgery, there is always a chance that things can go wrong. You could come through the operation but be unable to see or speak or even think clearly. Or you could lose the use of an arm or leg. Or you could hemorrhage and die during surgery. These are all possibilities, but very unlikely. Your surgeon is very experienced, he's done hundreds of operations like this."

She stared at his perfect hands while he spoke, then signed the form without reading it. When he'd left, she turned off the light near her bed and tried to pray, but her mind churned.

How will I be changed after tomorrow? If I come out of it not able to think clearly, what will I do with the rest of my life? What if I can't write or read? What if I come out of it feeling that my vocation was as false as my visions?

Low clouds had blown in from the ocean and absorbed the light from the nearby freeway lamps, turning the sky a murky purplish orange. The color of sacrifice.

Into Thy hands.

Vincent de Paul, Priest

When a nurse came in to get her at six, Sister John was more relieved than anxious.

"I'll give you an injection now, Sister."

Everything in the room softened. A familiar face appeared. "Good morning," Dr. Sheppard said. "Today's your tune-up."

She felt glad to see him. The drugs made her feel giddy. "I smell coffee," she said.

"I wish I could give you some, but it'll have to wait."

She studied his face. His features reminded her of the portrait of the young Saint Augustine hanging in the scriptorium—studious, exhausted, determined. He promised to see her in a few hours.

The nurse helped her change into a gown as white as the bridal dress she had worn at her Clothing Ceremony, then she lay down on a gurney. An orderly with mahogany skin and a gray mustache pushed the gurney out of the room and down the hallway toward the elevator. He hummed a tune as he pushed, and Sister John began to feel as if she were riding the music rather than a metal cart.

They hummed down a yellow corridor, then a green one. White uniforms smeared out in time as they hummed past, then they changed to the same green as the walls. Surgical scrubs. The ceiling turned to white tile. An overhead light was so bright it looked dark.

More green uniforms closed in. Someone lowered a mask over her face and told her to breathe normally. All she could see of this person were his eyes.

She shrank to a little point and blinked off.

Vines? Rigging of a ship? Sea snakes?

Tubes.

Colored lights, monitors, beeping sounds.

Sister Mary Michael and Mother Emmanuel, chatting with a nurse.

"Would a cloned human being have a soul?"

"God would find a way."

The nurse pointed out that identical twins were already clones in a sense, and Mother Emmanuel suggested that the soul to worry about belonged to the person who would have himself cloned at great expense when so many unwanted children were going hungry.

Drawn blinds.

Would a community of nuns cloned from a single Sister get along perfectly? If two cloned Sisters became infatuated with each other, what would you call that?

Sister John fell asleep again.

Dr. Sheppard visited her several times that day to monitor her recovery, assuring her and her brown-robed visitors that the operation had gone exactly as planned. Sister Mary Michael and Mother Emmanuel stayed by her side until it got dark outside, then promised to return the next morning.

For two days Sister John drifted in and out of sleep, feeling peaceful but disconnected from everything going on around her. On the third day she woke up feeling sore all over. A priest gave her communion before breakfast, but when she tried to read from the Office after the doctors' morning rounds, she found that she could not concentrate well enough to take the words to heart.

Father, you cut down the unfruitful branch for
   burning and

prune the fertile to
make it
bear
more fruit.

Dr. Sheppard assured her that this was normal. Heeding his advice, she began walking up and down the corridors for exercise, rolling her IV frame alongside her. One hallway window offered a view of the plaza linking the main hospital to other buildings associated with the medical center. The tiny human figures below, most of them in white jackets and green scrubs, streamed across the plaza in well-worn paths. It looked like the courtyard of a large monastery, she thought, only with the action speeded up. Instead of breviaries and rosary beads, the doctors carried patient charts and hot beverage cups.

She watched a team of residents, led by an attending physician, go into a nearby room and interview a stroke victim. Listening in to their discussion, Sister John inferred another parallel between religious life and the culture of medicine: the spirit of obedience ruled in the hospital, as it did in the cloister. Younger doctors yielded without hesitation to the will of their superiors, as if hoping to become perfect vessels for the greater will of medicine. Cooperation and teamwork were more important than individual achievement.

She wondered if a doctor, visiting a monastery, would draw

the same parallels. Or would he translate the experience into the language of pathology? The ideal of continual prayer: *hyperreligiosity.* The choice to live as a celibate: *hyposexuality.* Control of the will through control of the body, achieved through regular fasting: *anorexia.* Keeping a detailed spiritual journal: *hypergraphia.* None of these terms troubled her as deeply, however, as the one she brought from her own tradition: *spiritual pride.* She was convinced now that her epilepsy had been merely an opportunistic virus; egotism had weakened her resistance to it.

Like her doctor, she had dedicated her life to the service of others, but had she really been of service to anyone? She had vowed to lead a life of charity, but in fact she had been dependent on others' charity all along, and was even more dependent now that she was in the hospital. And what about the future? Her treatment for epilepsy would define her for the rest of her life. No matter what she did in the cloister from now on, it would always be followed by an asterisk and questions about the nature of her relationship to God.

Am I really a person who lives by faith? God can surely tell the difference between someone who walks in darkness and someone who walks with her eyes shut. Which am I?

Thérèse of the Child Jesus, Virgin and Doctor

Before dawn, she lit a votive candle on the tray next to her hospital bed and prayed the responsory in Thérèse's honor:

> *From the very beginning, O God, You came to me with*
> *Your*
> > *love,*
> *which had grown since my childhood.*
> *Its depths I cannot fully grasp.*

Saint Thérèse, whose only ambition had been to love, was now a Doctor of the Church. This was history, and Sister John had almost become part of it by participating in the ceremony at the Vatican; instead, she was reading the Office alone in a hospital bed. This was like childhood, but not the spiritual childhood Saint Thérèse advocated. This was Sister

John's own childhood all over again: feeling desperate and in need of rescue, but suspecting that the rescue party was no longer interested.

Afire with shafts of holy love she turned
From earthly joys to yearn for those of heav'n;
Eternal triumph now her soul's reward!

Every Carmelite monastery in the world was linked, through prayer, to the ceremony at the Vatican. Understandably, Mother Emmanuel was too busy to visit the hospital that day. Sister John was relieved when Sister Mary Michael came alone; she did not want to talk about the day or its significance, and there would have been no avoiding it had the prioress been there. Instead, she asked Sister Mary Michael what had led her to become a Carmelite extern after being married and raising children. Had she felt a calling for a long time, or had it appeared suddenly?

"A little of both," the extern answered, unwrapping a loaf of Sister Christine's walnut bread. "I loved being a mother, but once our kids were grown, I needed something else. I didn't want to become one of those women who only live in the past; I wanted to be of use. I did volunteer work through the Church for a while, but when my husband passed away, I felt the need to make a deeper commitment. I looked into becoming an extern, and this community seemed to need me the most.

"I'm not like you cloistered Sisters, whose vocations burn so bright. I couldn't spend all those hours in choir, my mind wanders too much. It's enough for me just to feel the strength of your prayers and to see the effect you have on the parishioners, who have become like family to me. How many people get to have as varied a life as I've had? I wouldn't change a thing about it."

"It may be that your vocation burns the brightest of all," Sister John said. "You've always felt you were where you belonged. I wish I could say the same."

Sister Mary Michael waved the compliment away. "I feel that way now, but that's hindsight. Nobody raising three kids knows any certainty, believe me. And anyway, you're too young to be thinking about peace of mind, you're still in the middle of your journey. Christ hardly knew any peace—he struggled right up to the end. There's your model."

Guardian Angels

"Time to have a look." Dr. Sheppard supported her neck with his left hand while he unwound the cotton strip with his right. When the bandage had been completely removed, his left hand stayed on her neck for just a moment as he inspected the wound. When he pulled it away, the cool air sent a shiver down her back.

"Looks good." He opened up a nearby drawer and took out a pair of miniature pliers. "I'm going to take out the staples now. This might hurt, but only for a second."

He removed them so quickly that she hardly felt anything. He swabbed the wound with an alcohol-based disinfectant—sending another chill down her spine—then wrapped a fresh bandage around her head. He pressed the cotton strip down with one hand and trimmed it with a pair of surgical scissors. As he fastened the bandage with tape, he held the scissors in his mouth, his lower lip yielding to the weight of the tiny instrument.

"It would be a good idea if you didn't shave your head for a while," he said, dropping the scissors into a wastebasket. "We don't want to risk an infection near that wound."

She asked why he had discarded the new-looking scissors.

"It's the law. We're not allowed to use them more than once without sterilizing them, and sterilizing is expensive. It's cheaper to buy new ones."

"Even if you only used them to snip a bandage?"

"That's right."

The thought of all that waste dismayed her. "Could I take that pair, then? We could get a lot of use out of them."

He bent down and recovered them for her. They were the sharpest scissors she had ever seen. He sat down facing her, and smiled. "Your EEG came out clean. I think we've got this thing licked."

She tried her best to smile back.

He did not appear surprised by her subdued reaction. "Don't worry about it if you feel a little washed out. Almost all patients experience some postsurgical depression, especially after this kind of surgery. Life without seizures may seem a bit dull at first, but that's a normal adjustment."

A normal adjustment? For three astonishing years she had lived and prayed from the inside of a kaleidoscope. Everything fit into a design of feeling, a pattern linking all souls and minds together. She felt God's presence in the design, and nothing seemed out of place. Every person was like a piece of glass in a giant rose window. Now the pattern was gone.

"In religious life," she said, turning the scissors over in her palm, "if you lose confidence in your personal experience, it's hard to keep from doubting everything."

He closed the manila file containing her charts. "That's true for everybody, isn't it? I nearly quit medicine during my first year of residency because I realized I'd gotten into it for the wrong reasons. But here I still am, and I'm glad I stuck with it."

She appreciated hearing something personal from him. "What kept you going?"

He laughed. "Finding out that *everybody* gets into medicine for the wrong reasons. It seems to come with the territory."

Francis of Assisi

On Sister John's last day at the hospital, an unconscious patient, a teenage girl, was wheeled into her room on a gurney, her head completely wrapped in bandages. A machine breathed for her, and from the demeanor of the orderlies bringing her in, Sister John guessed she was gravely injured. Dr. Sheppard arrived shortly afterwards and pulled the curtains around the patient's bed to examine her. He left the room looking tired, then came back with a grief-stricken woman with two young daughters and a teenage son. The mother spoke Spanish, but the children answered her in English. The daughters clung to their mother while the brother sat apart from them all and glared at the floor. He looked about fifteen.

Sister John approached the family and asked if there was

anything she could do to help. The mother didn't understand her, the son ignored her, and the daughters were either too young or too upset to know how to respond. When Sister John stepped into the hallway to give the family some privacy, she nearly bumped into a police officer standing outside the door to their room.

It was nearly dark out. She sat on the ledge of the window across from the nurses' station and watched as an ambulance, lights flashing and siren wailing, exited the freeway and sped toward the hospital. She dreaded going back to the room. She tried to pray for the injured girl, but something was missing. She couldn't feel her way to a connection with God the way she had in the past.

A patient's bell went off somewhere down the hall. Another ambulance exited the freeway and disappeared into the receiving bay, five floors down.

"Look at that," someone said. She turned and saw Dr. Sheppard standing a few feet away, gazing out the same window. The moon had just risen above the horizon to the east, appearing twice its normal size. "It looks fake, like a billboard. Or some new Disney stunt."

She tugged at the sleeves of her hospital gown until they covered her forearms.

"I wish we could move you to another room," he said, still looking out the window, "but it gets busy here on weekends. We had no other place to put her."

"I don't mind. It's a hospital."

He took out a pack of gum and offered her a piece. She declined. "What happened to her?" she asked.

He put a stick of gum in his mouth, then rubbed his neck as if trying to massage a cramp. "She got shot in the head. Not a good thing."

"Is she going to live?"

"The survival rate for the injury isn't high."

His retreat into jargon chilled her. "What's the policeman for?"

"Apparently the patient was involved in a crime at the time of the shooting. The guard is there to be sure she doesn't walk out of the hospital and disappear." He sighed. "You don't have to be Oliver Sacks to know that's not going to happen."

From down the hallway, the patient's bell went off again, this time more insistently. A night nurse sauntered by, but not in the direction of the patient's room. Dr. Sheppard groaned and pushed away from the window.

Sister John thought about what Sister Mary Michael had said the previous day about Christ knowing no peace, and having to struggle to the end. At times, reality had taken even him by surprise.

Seventeenth Sunday in Ordinary Time

Sister John took her folded habit out of the closet and changed in the bathroom. Tunic, scapular, sandals. Her veil didn't fit properly over the bandage; she would have to fix it when she got back to the monastery. She read through Lauds while the grieving mother slumped in a chair next to her daughter's bed. Before breakfast, Dr. Sheppard came into the room with a Spanish-speaking intern. They pulled the curtains shut around the bed to speak to the mother.

Sister John could not hear what was said, but from the sound of the woman's reaction, it must have been terrible news to deliver. The agonized consultation seemed to go on forever, then the curtain slid open and the two doctors left. Sister John saw the intern lean against the wall in the hallway. Dr. Sheppard touched her shoulder and spoke to her quietly.

A pair of orderlies entered the room with a gurney. Dr.

Sheppard followed them in and helped as they moved the unconscious girl and her breathing apparatus onto it. When one of her arms slid out from under the sheet, looking momentarily animated, the mother became frantic. Dr. Sheppard had to hold her back as one of the orderlies tucked the girl's arm under the sheet, treating it as gently as if it were attached to someone conscious. Sister John looked down at her own hands and saw they were shaking.

The gurney left the room with the mother walking beside it. Dr. Sheppard stayed behind to gather her charts.

"Where is she going?" Sister John asked.

He didn't answer directly. "We're giving the family some time with her first." He rearranged the papers in her file several times. "It's going to be a tough morning." He started massaging his neck again, then seemed to notice for the first time that Sister John was in habit again, ready to go home. "But I get to see you walk out of here with no symptoms. That makes it a good day." He tucked the papers under his arm, then said, "Hold on a second. I have something for you." He left the room and came back with a box labeled GAUZE ROLLS.

"Will I need these?" she asked.

"Look inside."

She opened the box and saw that it was filled with pairs of scissors, all different shapes and sizes.

"Now you and your Sisters won't have to fight over that other one."

Facing the lab coat while in her habit, she felt like a frontier guard saying good-bye to her counterpart across the border. She thanked him and wished him God's peace, then stepped into the elevator. When the doors slid closed, she saw her own image in the polished metal surface. The garment she had cherished for so long looked strange, like a costume.

1997

Faith

Teresa of Avila,
Virgin and Doctor

Orion leaned toward the ocean, fleeing the smudge of light over the mountains. Muffled wingbeats: a band of crows in formation, on their way to a landfill for the morning's harvest. Instead of cries, they made rattling sounds in their throats.

Sister John turned on the lights in the infirmary and offered the day to God:

Anyone who is lukewarm in his work is close to falling.

She dressed quietly. The wound over her ear had closed, but her heart gaped. Her doctor was right—life after epilepsy seemed dull. She felt as if she had tumbled out of a sacred mountain into a ruined village. The cloister buildings looked institutional, her Sisters' piety showed signs of wear, and the psalms read like the libretto of an opera delivered as a speech.

God's presence was replaced by an atmosphere of human compromise. Her convalescence in the infirmary became a prolonged examination of conscience.

Throughout the cloister, spiritual quotations had been painted over doorways to keep the Sisters' minds on God during the ordinary, in-between moments of daily life. These messages tended to become invisible over time, but now the one over the infirmary door would not disappear even when Sister John turned her back to it:

> *If I serve Thee in hopes of Paradise,*
> *deny me Paradise.*
> *If I serve Thee in fear of hell,*
> *condemn me to hell.*
> *But if I love Thee for love of Thyself,*
> *then grant me Thyself.*

She had come to the cloister in hopes of paradise; proof of it was how disillusioned she had become in the years after Solemn Profession, when the novelty wore off and paradise still eluded her. She reacted out of fear, shutting down her emotions and losing herself in busywork disguised as service to God. Her readiness to interpret her seizures as spiritual favors rather than signs of illness: renewed hopes of paradise. Deciding on surgery out of a sense of obligation: fear of hell.

In the next bed, Sister Teresa was all white hair, parched skin, and staring eyes. She hardly spoke anymore, but when she did, it was usually to people no one else could see. In this least favorite room of the monastery, endurance passed for reverence, prayer veered toward bargaining, and cleanliness substituted for purity. Even the furniture acknowledged defeat: beds with railings, doughnut-shaped cushions, wheelchairs, a chrome-plated walker. While the cross in each nun's cell issued a challenge to love, the one in the infirmary offered the consolation of surrender.

I'm too young to feel finished, too old to start over, and too worn out to see coherence in all this. How many times can a person fail before losing heart? Forgive me, Lord.

Fog rolled up through the canyon and over the cloister wall, so thick that even Saint Joseph disappeared into the void. Sister Miriam entered with a breakfast tray, bowing at the foot of Sister John's bed before serving her.

A nun in the infirmary shall be looked upon as Christ.

This lesson, like so many in the education of a Carmelite, addressed the problem of how to turn an unpleasant task—in this case, caring for a sick nun—into an opportunity for grace. Nothing in the training, however, prepared the sick nun for the role of the Beloved. Sister John did not enjoy being looked upon as Christ because she knew she did not resemble Christ at all. The bandage on her head was more dunce cap than halo.

"Praised be Jesus Christ."

"May He be forever praised. How was Father Aaron's sermon this morning?" Speech was allowed in the infirmary, where charity took priority over obedience. Sister John thanked God for that; any distraction from her own thoughts was welcome now.

Sister Miriam set the tray down. "I liked it. He talked about how, even for Saint Teresa, things never got easy." She sprinkled raisins and cinnamon on Sister John's oatmeal, poured milk on it, then buttered her toast for her.

Sister John watched guiltily, knowing that Sister Miriam had eaten only cold cereal for breakfast. She tried the oatmeal, but couldn't taste anything; since the operation, her sense of smell had all but disappeared. "Are you feeling better since your parents' visit?" she asked.

Sister Miriam brushed her veil away from her cheek. "I had a long talk with Mother Emmanuel, like you suggested. I told her about having days where I don't feel sure." She pursed her lips. "About belonging here, I mean."

"And what did Mother Emmanuel say?"

"That she has days when she doesn't feel sure, either. Even now." Sister Miriam looked up hopefully. "She said that no matter how many times we hear what it costs to follow Christ, we're still shocked when the bill comes, and we wonder all over again if we can pay it. If we make an act of faith then, it counts more than on the days when we feel sure."

Sister Miriam got up to check Sister Teresa's feeding tube and change the towel under the old woman's chin. The fog had lifted outdoors to reveal a clay-white sky. "What about temporary vows?" Sister John asked. "Do you feel ready?"

"I don't have it all worked out, but I'm ready. I want to try working with what I've got instead of wishing I had something else."

The sound of the wooden clapper carried from the refectory. Sister Miriam bowed again, but paused before leaving. "I want to thank you for talking to me that day," she said. "It helped a lot."

"You'll do the same for me one day, I'm sure."

Sister Miriam smiled, then passed under the quote on her way out. Silence took her place in the room, and Sister John felt marooned in it. A red-tailed hawk settled on one of the eucalyptus trees beyond the cloister wall, but was not able to enjoy peace there for long. A pair of mockingbirds, each a fraction of the hawk's size, lunged and screamed at it until the hawk flew off. The mockingbirds gave chase until the giant had disappeared, then returned to their spot in the ginkgo tree.

Sister Teresa mumbled at the ceiling, neck stretched and hands retracted as if she were clutching a purse. Sister John thought: There's someone who knows what it costs to follow Christ. She gave God everything she had, and now she doesn't even know who she is, much less that she was a nun.

During private prayer after Vespers, Mother Mary Joseph shuffled into the infirmary with a basket. Her body was curved into the shape of a question mark. She uncovered the basket and held a popover roll in front of Sister Teresa, who became alert all of a sudden and grinned like a child. Mother Mary Joseph fed her by hand until she had eaten nearly half a roll, then brought the basket over to Sister John.

"Resting well?" the Living Rule asked. It came out as more of a squeak than a question.

"I'm looking forward to getting back to choir. I feel useless in here."

Mother Mary Joseph pointed to Sister Teresa. "You're keeping her company." The former prioress took a moment to admire the garden through the window, then asked, "Written anything?"

Sister John pointed to her bandage. "When they took this out, my muse went with it."

"God must think you did enough with that gift. Now he wants you to do something else."

"That's a positive way of looking at it."

Mother Mary Joseph brushed the crumbs out of the basket into her palm. "What other way is there?" She crossed the infirmary, opened the window, and tossed the crumbs out to where the birds could eat them. She was barely able to reach over the windowsill. "Christ died without seeing his work completed," she said. "By human standards he was a failure, but faith turned his defeat into victory. How he looked at it was everything."

She returned to her spot next to Sister John's bed. "God showed you what heaven could be like, and you shared it with others. Now you can do something even better."

"You think so?"

Mother Mary Joseph nodded from the waist. "Walk in faith even though heaven seems out of reach. Think how good it would be if you could write about that."

Leaves dropped from the ginkgo tree like gold coins, mocking Sister John's poverty. It was one thing to be poor in spirit, like Christ, but another to be poor in faith. "I need to *read* that book, not write it," Sister John said.

Mother Mary Joseph shook her head. "Everything we learn about God leads to deeper mystery. Hard to accept sometimes, but we have to keep going." The old nun's voice was ready to give out. She squinted and eyed the wall. "What does that clock say?"

"Five-twenty."

She frowned and gathered her basket. "Too much talk. Pray for the next batch of rolls."

All Saints

With veils pulled forward to cover their faces, the nuns stood in choir, holding candles as Mother Emmanuel delivered the opening prayer:

When we make our vows, we hold out all that we are or may become to You.

Sister Miriam appeared at the far end of the room, wearing her novice's white veil for the last time. Her novice mistress, Sister Elizabeth, had been given the honor of calling for her at the hermitage and leading her as far as the door to the choir, but Sister Miriam had to make the journey to the altar alone.

As Sister John watched, she recalled the joy and certainty she had felt during her own ceremony, so many years ago.

Everything had seemed clear then; she was falling toward God like a stone falling toward the sun. Instead of plunging into the sun's heart, however, she had missed and been cast back into a vacuum. Her path was not to be a straight line after all, but a comet's ellipse.

Sister Miriam walked slowly, making it look like a natural pace. With each step she seemed to say: Here I am, as I am, as God made me. When she reached the altar, Mother Emmanuel bowed and pointed to two squares of cloth laid out before the tabernacle. One was white and represented the world. The other was black, representing the walk through darkness that all contemplatives make. Mother Emmanuel's lips barely moved as she whispered something for only the two of them to hear, then she stepped aside.

Sister Miriam extended her right hand and lowered it onto the black cloth, then knelt down with her hands stretched out in front of her, palms up. Mother Emmanuel came forward to adjust them so that one hand caught the light from the window, while the other was in shadow, then said to the gathering, "We stretch out our emptied hands to take hold of the Light of Christ. We ask that His Holy Spirit animate us with His love and life, but we know, in faith, that often we do not *feel* animated. We come to the cloister hoping that God's will and our own may be joyfully reunited, but find instead that we are more aware than ever of the gap between them. We may feel that our prayers are arid, or that we have lost our way, or that God has abandoned us. Although we suffer deeply, those become our most precious hours here, because only in complete darkness do we learn that faith gives off light.

"Sister Miriam, do you promise obedience, chastity, and poverty to God for the next three years, according to the primitive Rule of the Order of Discalced Carmelites?"

"I do."

"Do you make these vows of your own free will?"

"I do."

Sister Miriam lay facedown on the floor, her arms outstretched in the form of a cross, while Sister John helped cover her with a white sheet. This was the sign of the mystical death through which the nun promises to die to the world and to self. Sister John raised her eyes from the ceremony to look out the window of the choir. The trees were all reaching upward. They would die without ever touching the sun, but in the meantime they provided shade, beauty, and oxygen. When they fell, they would nourish the next generation of trees.

The prioress struck a wooden clapper and, one at a time, the nuns stepped forward to slide a piece of paper under Sister Miriam's body. These were intention slips; tradition held that a new bride of Christ was especially close to God at that moment, and that her requests were certain to be heard. On her own slip, Sister John had written the names of her half-siblings and a prayer for faith.

During the prostration, while the community chanted the

hymn *Veni Creator Spiritus,* they asked that the Holy Spirit strengthen, guide, and protect them; they prayed for their monastery and for its benefactors, and they prayed for the salvation of all mankind. The hymn ended, and in the silence that followed, Sister John remembered her very first prayer at Carmel, when Mother Mary Joseph told her to kneel before the altar and make her wishes known to God.

Please, God, let me know you.

If God's mystery only deepens as we learn about him, she thought, then maybe he's been answering my prayer after all.

The white sheet was removed and Sister Miriam rose. Mother Emmanuel lifted the novice's veil from her head and replaced it with the veil of Profession, then turned her around to face the others. Sister Miriam's face looked radiant, an effect heightened by the contrast between light and dark veil. The community sang the *De Colores* as they recessed to the courtyard, where Mother Mary Joseph passed out hand bells. The nuns circulated through the garden like fireflies, their bells tiny beacons of sound, wishing each other God's peace as they laughed and reminisced and wondered aloud when God might call the next woman to Carmel. She was out there somewhere; could she be hearing the voice of the Other at this very moment?

Sister Miriam had been hugged so often that her new veil, fastened hastily during the ceremony, had been pulled askew, making her look slightly drunk. Sister Anne wanted to straighten it for her, but Sister Elizabeth shooed her off. Sister Angelica kept her eyes on everyone's feet; she worried that, in all the excitement, one of the revelers might step off the flagstones and threaten the miniature life of the garden. Mother Mary Joseph excused herself to share the good news with Sister Teresa in the infirmary, while Sisters Christine and Bernadette talked about how to deal with the noise problem once the roofers began construction.

Sister John stopped by the fountain and saw that leaves had nearly clogged the filter leading to the pump. As she cleared them away with a stick, Mother Emmanuel approached and whispered, "I don't know who looks happier—Sister Miriam or Sister Elizabeth. That was a difficult novitiate."

"She wasn't allowing herself to be human," Sister John said. "I'm glad she talked with you about it. She seems much more relaxed now."

Mother Emmanuel looked pleased. "I tried to reassure her that her feelings were normal. We all have to *try* to become holy on our own, and fail, before we can approach God with humility."

The bells set the canaries off, turning the garden into a rain forest.

"Which got me to thinking about Claire Bours," Mother Emmanuel continued. "She'll be arriving next month. She's a bright girl, used to succeeding when she sets her mind to it; I worry that she'll have trouble adjusting to the fact that she can't force God to come to her. She'll need a novice mistress with a special understanding of the difficulties we face trying to do God's will." The prioress's eyes were the same color as the sky. "My heart tells me you would be the right person."

Sister John could see in through the window of the infirmary. Sister Teresa, her own novice mistress, was just out of view. "I don't feel I know anything about God's will, Mother."

"Yet you're still here, trying to do His will anyway. That's the kind of understanding I meant. The doing kind, not the knowing kind."

Neither of them spoke for a while. Sparrows drawn by the commotion in the garden called down from the trees. They seemed to have the best kind of understanding of all; they answered yes to everything.

"I'll do my best, Mother."

A group had formed at the Blessed Virgin's shrine to pay respects. Mother Emmanuel left to join them, but Sister John stayed behind to finish clearing the fountain. When she got the water flowing properly, she stepped back, took her bell out of her pocket, and rang it. The sound cheered her, then vanished into the deep blue air, which seemed to go on forever.

A NOTE ON THE AUTHOR

Mark Salzman is the author of
Iron & Silk, an account of his two years
in China, the novels *The Laughing Sutra*
and *The Soloist*, which was a finalist for
the *Los Angeles Times* Book Prize
for fiction, and *Lost in Place*, a memoir.
He lives in Los Angeles with his wife,
filmmaker Jessica Yu.